W9-AMO-968

Con Affetto,
With

Love,

Sabrina ♡

Sabrina ☺

Katy

Katy

Mary Evelyn Notgrass

Illustrated by the Author

Notgrass History
Gainesboro, Tennessee
notgrass.com

Text and Illustrations Copyright © 2005, 2011, 2017
by Mary Evelyn Notgrass McCurdy
Cover Background Image by BK0808 / Shutterstock.com

No part of this publication may be reproduced in any form
without written permission from the publisher.

ISBN 978-1-60999-112-8
Printed and Bound in the United States of America

Contents

Dedicated with love to my dear friend,
Irene Anderson.
I pray that God will make me like you some day.

Katy

1

The Light Bulb

Katy Porter woke up and stretched as hard as she could, pressing her hands against the headboard. She threw off the lightweight pink and blue quilt her mom had made and sat up. As she did, her head hit the top bunk, waking up Anna.

"Ouch!" Katy exclaimed, rubbing the top of her head.

"Are you all right, Katy?" Anna asked. Katy looked up at her sister's face peering over the railing of the top bunk. Anna's long brown hair tickled Katy's face. She laughed, despite the bump that was forming on her head.

"Anna, that tickles!" Katy laughed and scratched her tingling nose.

"You think that tickles?" said Anna as she climbed down the ladder. "How about this?" Anna leaped onto Katy's bed and began to tickle her sister. Katy screamed and then started laughing. She was laughing so hard she could barely breathe and she had little strength to resist her sister. Katy finally managed to utter the word, "Stop!" Anna pulled her arms away. The two sisters lay side by side on Katy's bed, panting and laughing.

"I guess we should get up," Anna said, still panting. "It's your turn to feed the fish."

"Oh, good!" said Katy. "I like the way those little flakes of fish food feel in between my fingers when I sprinkle them over the water. Don't you? It's like stiff tissue paper or something."

Anna laughed. "I guess I never really thought about it; but you know, it does feel pretty neat!" Anna climbed back up the ladder to make her bed. Her quilt was pink and blue, too, just like Katy's.

Katy sat up, careful not to bump her head again, and made her bed. She carefully laid her favorite doll on her pillow. Sugar Plum still wore the blue dress and white apron she had worn when Katy received her as a gift on her first birthday. The Velcro was worn out on her dress, so it never stayed fastened very long. Sugar Plum had a patch on her neck where her head had started to fall off. She had a patch on each arm and one on each of her cloth shoes. The elastic on her sleeves was worn out, too. No matter how many times Katy pulled down on them, they always crept back up to make the doll's long-sleeved dress a short-sleeved one. Sugar Plum's face and hair were dirty, but Katy liked her better that way.

Katy walked over to the fish tank on the dresser. "Good morning, Wiggly Worm!" she said to her goldfish. Katy picked up the container of fish food and unscrewed the lid. She wrinkled her nose. She liked the way the flakes felt, but despised the way they smelled. She got a pinch of fish food and sprinkled it in the tank. She watched as Wiggly Worm swam to the top for his breakfast. Incognito, Anna's goldfish, soon followed.

"Anna?" Katy said to her sister in as sweet a voice as she could manage. "Will you go to the Acorn Lady's house with me? We could get dressed and go on before breakfast if it's okay with Mom."

The Acorn Lady was an elderly woman who lived down the street from the Porters. A massive oak tree grew in her front yard. One year, Mom had asked her if she would give the Porters permission to gather the acorns that fell to the ground. Mom liked to use them for craft projects. The Acorn Lady had gladly given them permission and told them they could come any time they pleased.

"No, I don't really want to," Anna answered. "Besides, it's not fall. The acorns aren't ripe yet. Let's go in our playhouse instead." Katy thought that sounded like a good alternative. Still in their nightgowns, the two girls opened the door into their playhouse. The playhouse was a small closet in the girls' room. It had two platforms. From the second platform a ceiling entrance opened into the attic. Anna and Katy had claimed this closet as their playhouse soon after they moved to this part of Urbana, the Illinois town that had been Katy's home for as long as she could remember.

Katy climbed to the second platform and pulled the string that turned on the light bulb hanging from the ceiling. Anna suggested they draw more pictures to tape up on the walls. Anna was ten, two years younger than their brother Seth, and she usually had an idea of what they should do. Katy got down the paper, markers, and tape from the wire baskets that hung on the wall. Anna drew a puppy. She made it white with black spots. At the top, she wrote "Sparky."

"That's what I'll name my dog if I ever get one," she said. Anna had talked about wanting to get a dog for years. Katy drew a tree with a swing hanging from it. It looked like the swing which hung from the crabapple tree in their front yard. Katy loved that swing. It was simply a piece of wood with a notch cut in each end. A pink rope wrapped around the seat and was tied to a branch overhead. A friend at church had given them the swing the summer before. Katy liked to swing as hard as she could and then jump out onto the grass.

When the drawings were finished, the girls taped them to the wall beside ones they had drawn the day before.

"Whew!" said Katy, as she wiped her sweaty forehead. It didn't take long for the playhouse to get stuffy during the summer. "It's hot! Let's go do something else." Anna was hot, too, so she agreed. As Katy and Anna were putting the art supplies away, Katy stood up suddenly without thinking about her surroundings. As soon as she stood up, the playhouse went black and glass shattered around them.

"My head!" Katy cried. Anna quickly opened the door, letting in the light from their bedroom so they could see. Mom rushed into the room.

"Katy!" she exclaimed. "What happened?"

"I stood up under the light bulb," Katy said, "and it broke." Katy was surprised that she wasn't crying, but it hadn't really hurt very much. It mostly scared her.

"Come on out here," said Mom. Katy came down out of the playhouse. Mom looked in Katy's hair. "Come on into the bathroom, Honey. You have some glass in your hair. I don't think your head is bleeding, though." Katy followed Mom into the bathroom. Mom opened a drawer and found a pair of tweezers. She began to pick out each tiny piece of glass in Katy's hair. Katy winced when her mom touched the bump on her head. She told Mom about hitting Anna's bunk.

"Your poor head," said Mom sympathetically. She continued to pull out bits of glass. After a few more minutes, Katy's mom announced, "Okay, Katy. Looks like you're all clean. Now you two run on, and I'll clean up the glass in your playhouse."

"Thanks, Mom," said Katy as she left the bathroom. She wandered into Seth's room and found him playing marbles on the floor. The summer before, Mom had stitched a large circle with yarn in an old scrap of carpet. The children used it as a marble ring.

"Is your head okay?" Seth asked his little sister.

"Oh, it's fine," answered Katy. "Can I play?"

"Sure, when I finish this game." Seth was pretending to be two people competing against each other. "It's Fred's turn now," he told Katy. "He's losing. The score is 3 to 5."

"What's the other guy's name?" Katy asked.

"I forgot. Look on the paper over there, and it'll say. I'm doing a whole tournament. Just look at who won the last game." Katy picked up the paper and scanned over the names. It was hard to read her brother's handwriting.

"Is it Yerry?" she asked.

"Yes," said Seth, "only it says Jerry, not Yerry."

"Well, your writing is so messy I couldn't tell," Katy said to herself. She decided not to say it out loud, though. Katy sat on the edge of her brother's bed as Seth played the last few innings of the game.

"Fred won after all," he announced.

Katy smiled. "I was for him all along."

As Seth began to set up a new game, Katy slid off the bed and joined him on the floor. They set up the thirteen marbles in an X in the center of the ring. Seth and Katy took turns trying to knock the marbles out of the ring with their shooters. Seth won, but Katy was used to that. It came with being eight years old and the youngest.

2

Homeschool?

"Kids," Dad said one evening at supper, "your Mom and I have something to talk with you about." Seth, Anna, and Katy looked at each other. Katy knew her father's tone. It didn't mean someone was in trouble, and it didn't necessarily mean bad news. It just meant that what he was about to say was serious and Katy needed to pay close attention.

"Mom and I are thinking about homeschooling the three of you this fall, instead of sending you back to public school." There was silence before Dad went on. "Public school didn't go too well last year. We had to pull Seth out of one of his classes because we didn't like what was being taught. We had problems with some of the teachers because they don't believe the way we do. You had some rough spots, too, didn't you, Katy?"

Katy nodded, thinking back over the previous year. Her teacher hadn't been very nice. She remembered the day one of the boys spit glue in her face. She thought about the bully who had been mean to her. She remembered some good times, but the bad times were there, too.

"We don't want to send you back to that," Mom said. "We want to protect you from the troublemakers and from the wrong things the teachers try to tell you. We haven't decided for sure, yet. We just wanted you to know we are thinking about it."

"What about my friends?" Anna asked.

"You can still see your friends at church and next door," Mom said. "We can work out times for you to see your school friends, too. Besides, think of all the homeschooled friends you can make."

"How will I meet them if we just stay at home?" Anna wanted to know.

"Homeschoolers go on field trips and picnics and have special classes together," Mom explained. "Just think about all that you can learn when you don't have to wait for the teacher to punish the bullies and wait for her to hand out 25 papers and wait in line. Besides, you'll get to be at home with Katy and Seth and me. We can be best friends. You won't have homework to do at night when Dad is home because you'll already have it done."

"We'll talk more about it. We aren't making the decision tonight; but Eva," said Dad, turning to his wife, "we do have to be at that meeting before too long."

"Okay, Jack," said Mom, getting up from the table. "Anna and Katy, I need you to clear the table so that we can get ready," said Mom as she began walking back to her bedroom. "Put the leftovers in the fridge, and I need you to load the dishwasher, too. There aren't many dishes."

"Yes, ma'am!" they called after her.

"What's this meeting for, anyway?" Katy asked Anna.

"It's something about a new committee or something at church," Anna replied. Katy took the last bite of her macaroni and cheese.

"Hey, Anna. Let's see how fast we can get it done so we can go play. Let's pretend we work in a diner and we have to do things really fast."

"Okay," Anna answered, "but we better not break anything. That would be bad!" Anna finished her macaroni. "Ready? Go!" The girls leaped up from the table and carried their plates into the kitchen, imagining they were waitresses, each wearing a white blouse and poodle skirt. When Anna and Katy had the table cleared, the dishwasher loaded, and the leftover macaroni in the refrigerator, their parents were still in their bedroom getting ready to leave. Seth was downstairs programming a new computer game. Seth liked to check out programming books from the public library. He spent hours at the computer creating moving pictures and games. Katy went to the top of the stairs.

"Seth!" she called down. "Want to go outside?"

"Sure!" came the reply. "I'll be up in a minute." Dad came down the hall straightening his necktie.

"There's no need to yell, Katy," he said. "If you want to talk to Seth you can go downstairs, okay?"

"Yes, sir," said Katy. As Dad walked back down the hall, Katy put on her red tennis shoes that were beside the back door. Anna slipped on her rainbow sandals. Dad and Mom walked into the room just as Katy opened the back door.

"Just a minute, girls," said Mom. "We're about to leave." She went to the top of the stairs and called down. "Seth, come on up! We're leaving."

"But, Dad," Katy blurted out, "you said we can't yell down the stairs!"

"I said you couldn't," said Dad firmly. "I didn't say anything about Mom." The thought, "It's not fair," came into Katy's mind; but she knew better than to say it out loud. She looked down at the blue carpet and her red tennis shoes, wishing she had kept her mouth closed. One lace had already come untied. As she bent down to double tie it, Seth came up the stairs, climbing three at a time.

"Okay, kids," said Mom, "we'll be at the Carrs' house. Seth is in charge until we get home."

"Just do what you're supposed to," Dad added. "It's fine to play outside, just be safe. We should be home about 9:00 and it will be off to bed after that." Dad and Mom kissed their children and told them goodbye. Katy, Anna, and Seth turned and raced out the back door. They ran to the playhouse at the back of the yard. Katy swung on the rope and Anna climbed up the rope ladder and sat on the top rung, swinging back and forth. Seth climbed up to the platform beside them. In a moment, the back door opened and Dad stuck his head out.

"Be smart," he called, "and come in when it gets

dark. Be careful, and no climbing trees while we're gone. Remember that Seth is in charge."

"Yes, sir!" the children called back in unison. Dad went back into the house and closed the door behind him. In a few seconds, they heard the minivan start and the garage door close.

"Homeschool?" said Anna, as she swung gently on the rope ladder. "Homeschool?"

"It sounds pretty good to me," Seth said casually. "You get to stay at home and learn more about what you want to learn about. You can learn at your own pace, too. I was bored stiff in math last year, because I already knew what the book was teaching. Maybe we could even stay in our pajamas all day!"

"Seth, you know there is no way Mom would go for that," said Anna. "I just don't know if I would like staying at home."

"I thought going to school was okay," Katy joined in, "but maybe this would be okay, too. I don't know. I don't want to be too different from everybody else. I would miss Ruth. We played together almost every day at recess. We caught a rolly-polly one time and named him Rolly. We put him in a tiny little box with some grass and kept it between the sidewalk and the school building. He lived at least one day."

"I'd miss my friends, too," said Anna, "and it's a little hard to picture Mom being our teacher." Anna leaned her head against one of the ropes of the rope ladder and stared off toward the house.

Seth and Katy decided to play baseball. Seth slid down the pole from the platform as Katy made one final swing on the rope and jumped off. Anna stayed on the rope ladder, still thinking.

Seth and Katy ran to the brown metal shed on the other side of the yard. The rusty door squeaked as Seth slid it open. He climbed over the lawn mower and picked through the spider webs. The plastic ball and bat were on a shelf at the rear of the shed. Seth emerged and threw the ball up into the air. He hit it with the bat and the plastic ball soared across the yard into a bush near the back door of the house. Katy ran after it and retrieved it from the scratchy branches. She turned around and saw Seth standing in batting position. She pitched the ball toward her brother, but it sailed far over his head.

"Not so hard," he said, picking up the ball and tossing it back to Katy. She threw the ball again, but this time it fell to the ground halfway between herself and Seth. Seth's shoulders sagged and he shook his head and sighed.

"I'm trying," whined Katy. "You said, 'not so hard.'"

"Well, it has to at least get to the bat," said Seth. He held the bat out flat beside him. "Throw it right here," he coached. Katy pitched the ball again. It still wasn't a very good pitch, but by taking two steps to the right, Seth managed to hit the ball. It flew into the air, onto the roof, and rolled down into the gutter.

"Oops," said Seth, smiling sheepishly. "I guess Dad will have to get that one. I'll see if I can find another." Seth turned and went back into the shed. He came out in a couple of minutes, brushing cob webs off his arms. "It has a crack, but I guess it'll do," he told his sister. "You want a turn to bat?" Katy nodded. Seth gently tossed her the plastic bat and Katy stood in position, ready to hit the ball. Seth pitched it perfectly; Katy swung and missed. On the fourth pitch she managed to hit the ball, but she hit it towards the ground and it didn't even make it all the way back to Seth. Discouraged, she let the bat drop and sighed.

"I'm no good," she said.

"You just need to practice some more," Seth replied. "You'll get it."

Katy shrugged and turned toward the playhouse at the back of the yard. "You can play by yourself if you want," she said. "I'm through."

Anna was still sitting on the rope ladder. "At least you hit it," she said as Katy walked near. "It takes me a gazillion pitches before I hit one." Katy shrugged again and climbed up to the platform of the playhouse. It cheered her up and made her laugh to watch Seth play

baseball by himself. He tossed the ball up, hit it with the bat, then dropped the bat and ran to catch the ball.

"What do you want to do?" Anna asked. "Do you want to play something?"

"Let's play castle," Katy answered. "The playhouse can be our castle."

"Okay," Anna agreed. "Do you want to both be princesses or what?"

"Yes, and let's have the enemy come and attack our castle and we have to run away to the forest to escape and live off berries and things."

"And a handsome prince can discover us and marry me," said Anna. She then quickly added, "And he can have a little brother, if you want."

As Anna and Katy planned their game, Seth hit the ball and caught it one last time. He put the ball and bat back in the shed and made his way across the yard to the back door of the house. "I'm going in," he called.

Anna and Katy looked at each other and each read the other's thoughts. Maybe they would rather play inside. It was one thing to play outside just the two of them when their parents were home; it was entirely different playing outside by themselves when just Seth was there. Anna and Katy raced each other to the back door and reached it just after Seth. "We're coming in, too," they told him.

Seth put his hand on the knob, but he didn't open the door.

"Come on, Seth, open it," Katy said impatiently.

"I can't," he replied, his hand dropping down to his side.

"What do you mean you can't?" asked Katy. "All you have to do is turn it like this." Katy put her hand on the doorknob and tried to turn it. "Oh," she said. "It's locked."

3

Locked Out

"Why would they lock us out?" Katy asked. "I don't get it!"

"I'm sure Dad just closed the door and then locked it without thinking," Anna tried to explain. "It's just a habit for them to close the door and lock it before they leave to go somewhere."

"But what are we going to do?" Katy said. She was getting worried. Seth and Anna looked at each other and shrugged. Katy sat down on the concrete step on which they stood. She put her elbows on her knees and rested her chin in her hands. Anna sat down beside her, and Seth sat down beside Anna. None of them knew what they should do. After a few moments of silence, Seth got up. "Where are you going?" Katy asked.

"At least we can check to see if maybe the other doors are unlocked," Seth answered. Katy and Anna got up, too. There was a door into the garage from the back yard. It was locked. Seth led the way over to the gate that led to the front yard. As they went through the gate, a thought suddenly came to Katy.

"Seth," she said, "how are we going to go inside before it gets dark like Dad said?"

"I think he'll be understanding," Seth answered. "After all," he added with a laugh, "he's the one who locked us out!" Seth opened the gate and they walked into the front yard. The garage door was closed. The side door into the kitchen was locked. They had only one more door to try. They walked around to the front door. Anna put her hand on the knob.

"It turns!" she said excitedly. She pushed, but the door didn't budge. The doorknob was unlocked, but the deadbolt above it wasn't.

The children turned and headed back around to the gate. No one said a word until the gate was closed behind them. Katy broke the silence by asking, "Why is it that the one time we need to use their phone they're out of town?"

"Whose phone?" Anna asked.

"Theirs." Katy pointed to the house next door. They were the only neighbors that the children knew well enough to ask for help. They were in Michigan, though, visiting grandparents. "Well, Seth," Katy asked slowly, "what do we do now?"

"I guess we wait for Dad and Mom to get home." The children stood still for a moment, glancing around at each other, at the ground, and at the back door. Anna finally asked Katy if she still wanted to play castle.

"I guess we might as well," Katy replied. The sisters walked slowly back to the playhouse and Seth went to the shed. He came out with a soccer ball and began kicking it up and down, back and forth, all across the yard. Every once in a while he kicked it between two of the metal posts in the middle of the chain link fence. "Aw, yeah!" he exclaimed every time, followed by, "Yesss."

Katy decided that her name would be Princess Leota. Anna wanted to be Princess Georgiana. The playhouse became their tower bedroom. From its windows they could see for miles across the rolling hills that surrounded their castle. Their mother had died of a rare disease when Leota was a baby. Their father, King

George, had become hard and mean and never wanted to see his daughters. Georgiana and Leota spent hours together in their room, in the stables, and in the forest that surrounded their enormous castle.

Anna thought it would be fun to pretend that a tutor taught them their lessons in one of the towers of the castle. They would go there every day and learn together.

"I guess we'll be homeschooled then, right?" asked Katy with a smile.

"I guess so," said Anna. "Maybe this homeschool thing could work out after all. We could be sort of like princesses." Katy liked the thought of that. "But I guess for now," Anna continued, "we should get on with the game." The girls' imaginations took them far away from their back yard.

"Leota, shall we go for a ride in the forest?" said Anna, pretending to be Georgiana with a proper, sophisticated voice.

"Yes, let's," Leota replied. The princesses lifted their beautiful silk skirts and descended the spiral staircase that wound down the inside of the tower. It was fun to imagine. The fact that their spiral staircase was really a wooden ladder didn't matter.

The girls reached the ground level of the castle and went out the back way. After crossing over the moat that encircled their home on an old wooden bridge, they walked side by side to the stable yard. They spoke of the strained relationship between their country and the land of Peria. They spoke of Peria's evil ruler, King Hiram, and the threats he had made toward their father.

"Do you think there will be a war?" Leota asked her older sister.

Georgiana sighed and said, "There has been tension between our people and the people of Peria for centuries. In the only war we have had against them, our armies won an overwhelming victory. I don't think Father will order an attack on them. If they attack us, they are sure to be defeated."

"I suppose so," Leota replied. They had by this time reached the stable yard. They greeted Benson, a character in their imaginations, who was the stable hand.

Georgiana's horse was white with a black mane and tail. Georgiana had named her Lotus. Leota's horse was black and had a white mane and tail. His name was Moonshadow. Moonshadow had a white blaze between his eyes.

Georgiana and Leota stepped into their changing room at the far end of the stable. Here were their riding habits and cloaks. They had no servants here to assist them as they dressed. They enjoyed helping each other and secretly wished that the servants in the castle would leave them alone.

After leading the horses from their stalls and saddling them, Georgiana and Leota each mounted her horse and rode off down the forest path.

At this point in their game, Anna and Katy galloped across the back yard on imaginary horses. Seth was still kicking his soccer ball. He kicked it toward his sisters and Katy kicked it back. When Seth again kicked the ball to them, Anna, no longer trying to sound important and royal, said, "Seth, please." She kicked the ball back to her brother, who again kicked it toward them.

"You'll make our horses fall, Seth," said Katy. She stopped riding her horse and rested her foot on the ball. Seth came to her, kicked the ball out from under Katy's foot, and rested his own foot upon it. "Whew, you're sweaty!" Katy said, wrinkling her nose. Seth's shirt was damp and his hair stuck to his head. He ran his fingers through his hair, making it stick up, and grinned.

"What are you guys doing anyway?" he asked.

"We're riding our horses through the forest," Katy answered.

Satisfied, Seth was off again, kicking the soccer ball. He kicked the ball into the fence, scoring another goal.

Georgiana and Leota rode on. They returned their animals to Benson at the stables and changed back into their imaginary silk dresses. They walked back to the

castle, arriving just in time for their royal dinner. They entered the castle and sat down at the long banquet table. In reality, Anna and Katy climbed up the ladder of the playhouse and sat across from each other on the wooden floor.

Georgiana and Leota each daintily laid her linen napkin in her lap. They picked up their shining, silver forks and savored the roast venison, steaming vegetables, and fresh bread. The crystal tinkled and the silver platters gleamed in the candlelight. King George sat at the head of the table.

Anna and Katy continued with their imaginings and didn't notice when Seth stopped kicking the soccer ball and put it back in the shed.

Georgiana gathered up courage and asked her father a question. "Father," she said, "are you concerned that there will be a war with Peria? Do you think they will attack us?" Anna deepened her voice and became King George.

"Georgiana, you have nothing to fear. King Hiram and all of Peria know to leave us be."

Anna changed her voice back to her own and spoke excitedly to Katy, "Okay, let's say that right now a servant rushes in and tells us that Peria is attacking. Pretend you say, 'We shall all perish,' and then you faint."

Katy drooped her shoulders and looked at Anna. "Don't say, 'Pretend you say,'" Katy whined. "Let me think of my own things to say."

"Okay," Anna replied. "I'm sorry. You can say whatever you want. Do you want to make the voice of the servant?"

"Sure," said Katy. She settled herself back into the game and then burst out, "Sire, the army of Peria is attacking! They are getting nearer to the castle every moment!"

"Rah-hah!" came a shout from beneath the playhouse. Anna and Katy screamed and jumped up. Seth appeared at the foot of the ladder, holding the yellow plastic baseball bat as if it were a sword. He cried out, "You are surrounded!" and climbed to the upper level of the playhouse.

"Leota, run!" Georgiana cried. Leota ran down the spiral staircase, Georgiana following close behind her.

"The king is captured!" cried the Perian soldier. "Now for his daughters!" Georgiana and Leota screamed again and the Perian soldier charged after them.

"You've no hope of escape," he warned. "The Perian army completely surrounds this castle." The soldier chased after the fleeing princesses and soon caught them. He led them to the dungeon of their own castle and locked them inside.

Anna and Katy sat down in the grass under the playhouse which served as the dungeon. Seth swung on the rope swing beside his prisoners. All three were quiet for several moments. Finally, Katy spoke up. "Have you guys realized how dark it's getting? When do you think Mom and Dad will be home?" She was getting a little scared. She looked up at the sky and saw the first stars of twilight begin to shine.

4

Scared

"It's going to be okay, Katy," said Anna. She put her arm around her sister's shoulders. "I see some lightning bugs. Why don't we go catch some?"

"I know you're just trying to cheer me up," said Katy.

"You're right," said Anna. They smiled at each other and Katy followed Anna out into the yard.

As they chased after the lightning bugs, Katy asked Anna, "So what about that handsome prince who was supposed to come and have a little brother?"

Anna thought a moment, and then answered, "I guess they came to our rescue and freed us from the dungeon and we got married in a double wedding and lived happily ever after." Katy nodded. She guessed so, too.

Seth returned his yellow plastic bat to the shed and came out with the small bug house made of wood and wire. The three of them filled it with lightning bugs. Soon it was too dark to catch any more. The mosquitoes were out and biting their arms, legs, and ankles. One bit Katy on the forehead. Eventually, the mosquitoes got tired of biting and the children got tired, too. They sat down in a circle on the grass. They put the bug house in the middle and stared at the lightning bugs. Katy was bored, but more than that, she was scared. It was dark.

"I wish Mom and Dad had left a light on in the house so we could see a little better," said Katy. The house looked deserted. Even the bathroom light was off. Twice, when a car came near, Katy thought it was their minivan, but both times the car drove on.

"Boy, I'm thirsty," said Anna.

"How about we get a drink from the hose?" Katy suggested.

"Good idea," Anna said. They all went over together and took a drink. After playing baseball and soccer, riding their horses through the forest, capturing a castle, being locked in a dungeon, and catching lightning bugs, the water tasted good. Its coolness washed away the

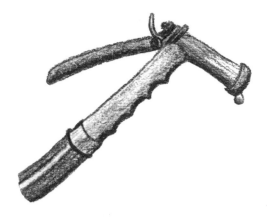

crusty feeling around Katy's lips and the sandy feeling in her throat. Katy wiped the sweat from her forehead and then put her face under the cold stream of water.

Seth, Anna, and Katy lay down in the grass and looked up at the stars. Since there weren't any lights on in the house, the stars seemed to shine brighter than usual.

"It's not that I'm necessarily scared of the dark," said Katy, "it's just that the doors are locked and we couldn't get in if we needed to. If Dad and Mom were here, I would think it would be cool to be out here like this. It's just kind of scary to be locked out of your own house at night." Anna reached over and patted her sister's leg. The grass tickled their legs and made their mosquito bites itch worse. Seth, Anna, and Katy climbed up the ladder of the playhouse and waited. Anna looked at her watch by the light of the moon that shone overhead.

"It's way past nine," she commented. "I wonder where they are."

"Oh, you know how it is," Seth replied. "They're probably just talking. They might have had to stop and get gas on the way home or something like that."

Katy felt tears in her eyes. She was glad it was dark so that Seth and Anna wouldn't see her crying. She didn't wipe the tears away or sniff because she didn't want them to know.

"So, do you think Dad and Mom will really decide to homeschool?" Seth asked.

"I don't know," said Anna. "I'm not sure if I want them to or not. I guess maybe it would be okay to give it a try. It's just hard to do something so unfamiliar, something I don't know about. I don't know any kids who are homeschooled, so it's hard to know what it would be like."

"Whatever we do," said Seth, "the final decision is up to Dad and Mom and they are going to do what they think is best."

Katy had remained silent while her brother and sister talked. Right at this moment, she didn't want to think about school; she wanted to go inside. The minutes dragged on. Finally, the children heard the garage door screech open.

"They're home!" all three cried at once. They ran around to the side of the garage.

"I wonder why all the lights are off," they heard their mom say. The children began to laugh as they burst through the gate.

"What are you doing outside?" Mom asked.

"You locked the door when you left and we couldn't get back in!" Katy told them.

"What?" Dad asked in surprise and confusion.

"You locked us out," said Anna. Dad unlocked the door and they all went inside. Katy scratched the bug bite on her forehead. The bite had become quite large.

"You poor thing!" said Mom, seeing the bite. She hugged Katy. It felt good to be safe in the house with her parents. Katy's eyes were still a little wet, but she didn't think anyone had noticed. As her mother held her close, Katy quickly wiped her eyes on her mother's blouse. The Porters sat down in the living room and Seth, Anna, and

Katy related their adventure in detail to their parents. When they had finished, Mom said it was time to take a quick shower and get to bed.

"And if you don't hurry," Dad added, looking straight at Katy, "the Tickle Monster is going to get you!" Katy squealed and ran down the hall. Her dad was right behind her. He gently tackled Katy on the floor of her bedroom and tickled until Katy had laughed so much she could hardly laugh any more.

"All right," said Dad, "now to the shower, Miss Katy-Batey. Oh, and Katy," he added before he left, "I'm glad that my big eight-year-old isn't too big for a chase from the Tickle Monster."

"I won't ever be too big," Katy assured him. She hurried to take a shower and brush her teeth. Before she climbed into bed, she peeked into Seth's room.

"I love you, Seth," she said.

"I love you, too," Seth replied.

Katy went to her room and crawled under the lightweight pink and blue quilt. She soon became hot and kicked it off. She hugged Sugar Plum and scratched the bite on her forehead.

When Anna was out of the shower, she came in and

flipped off the light. She climbed up the ladder and lay down on the top bunk. Dad and Mom soon came in to say good night.

"I sure am sorry we locked you out, girls," said Dad.

"It's okay, Dad," Katy replied. "It was kind of fun, even though I did get pretty scared."

"Mom?" Anna asked. "Have you talked any more about whether or not we are going to homeschool?"

"Dad and I talked about it some on the way home," said Mom. "There's no need to worry about it, Sweetie. We're praying about it and trying to make the right decision. It's a tough choice."

"You can pray about it, too, girls," Dad added. "It's been a long night, though, and it's time for you two to get some sleep." Dad said a prayer with Anna and Katy before he and Mom kissed their daughters and walked out into the hall. Katy heard them go down the hall and down the basement stairs. She thought they were probably going downstairs to talk about their tough choice. Katy prayed that they would make the right decision, whatever it was.

Katy lay in the darkness, her bug bites itching terribly. She started to laugh.

"What is it?" Anna asked.

"I was just thinking about how Seth locked us up in the game and how in real life we were locked up. We were just locked out instead of in!" Anna and Katy laughed together. Anna soon fell asleep. Katy was tired, but she couldn't get to sleep.

"What do you think, S.P.?" Katy whispered to her doll. "Will homeschooling make me too different?"

5

A Funny Smell

"Let's play olden days," Katy suggested to Anna one rainy afternoon. Their mom was in the kitchen making supper and Seth was in his room building a card house. Dad wasn't home from work yet.

"Okay! I'll go get the dress-up clothes from the basement," Anna said.

"How about we just play down there instead?" said Katy. "It's not as hot."

"Good idea. Come on!" Anna and Katy went downstairs and got out their dress-up box. Katy scratched the bug bite on her forehead. It was almost gone now, but it still itched occasionally.

Anna and Katy had one of the best dress-up collections of anyone they knew. They had skirts, aprons, hats, shoes, purses, jewelry, dresses, and shirts. They had their mom's old bridesmaid dresses from when she had been in the weddings of her friends. They had necklaces and hats given to them by elderly women at church. They even had some things that had once belonged to their great-grandmother.

Anna would be the mom, of course, and Katy would be her daughter. That's how it usually was when they played. "I'll be nine and my name will be Joan," Katy said, as she pulled on a pink skirt over her jeans. "And I have a big brother named Jonathan and a baby sister named Kathleen." Katy pulled a white blouse out of the dress-up box and put it on over her T-shirt.

"Okay, and our last name is Shlecker," said Anna, tying on a lavender apron over the green dress she had chosen. "I love the way your mouth feels when you say that. Shlecker," she repeated. "Shlecker." Anna got an old baby blanket. She put it on the small, blue plastic picnic table that had been a Christmas gift years before. Katy got out their plastic dishes and set them around the table. The dishes were green around the edges with flowers in the middle.

The Porters' basement was the perfect place to

play. Anna and Katy had hours of fun in it. It had an old kitchen counter with a stove and oven. The people who had lived in the house before the Porters moved there had remodeled the upstairs kitchen and put the old counters and appliances in the basement. The stove and oven weren't hooked up, so Anna and Katy played with them when they were in an orphanage, an office, or wherever their imaginations took them.

Anna began the game. "What did you say your name was, Katy?"

"Joan."

"Oh, yes. Come on, Joan. I need you to help me fix dinner."

"Coming, Mother!" Using their miniature pots and pans and their plastic food, Katy and Anna fixed a delicious dinner of turkey, peas, bread, and chocolate pie. Just as they were putting the last dish on the table, they heard someone coming down the stairs. They could tell by the footsteps that it was Seth.

"Seth," Katy said, "we're trying to play."

"Can't I play?" Seth asked.

"He did make it more exciting when we were playing castle outside," Anna said. "Let's give him a chance."

"Maybe he could be the big brother," Katy suggested.

"That's no good," Anna replied, "because he really is our big brother. He can be the dog." Seth agreed with a grin and got down on all fours.

"Here, Spot!" Katy called. "Here's your dog food!" Seth went over to the orange plastic plate that Katy put on the floor. He pretended to eat ravenously. Anna and Katy sat down at their table. As soon as they lifted their plastic forks to their mouths, Seth, as Spot, walked over on all fours, grabbed the baby blanket tablecloth in his teeth, and yanked it off, pulling all the plastic dishes with it.

"*Seth!*" Anna and Katy cried in unison. They both started to say something else when all of a sudden they noticed something strange.

"What's that funny smell?" Katy asked. Just then, they heard the smoke alarms upstairs. All three of the children jumped to their feet and hurried up the stairs. There was smoke everywhere.

"Mom?" they called.

"I'm in here," they heard from the kitchen. "It's okay. I forgot about the plastic containers I hid in the oven last night before our company came. I just turned on the oven and, well, you can see—" Mom's coughing broke off her sentence. The children peered into the oven and saw plastic bowls and lids hanging from the oven rack like icicles. "Open things up for me, kids," Mom managed to say. Seth, Anna, and Katy went through the house opening the doors and windows. By the time Dad came home from work, most of smoke was gone, but the smell still lingered. Mom told him all that had happened.

"Dad," said Katy when her mom had finished, "since it kind of smells bad in here, and since the rain has finally cleared off, could we go outside and play basketball together?"

Dad smiled. "Okay, Katy. I'll meet you outside after I change clothes. And I think you might want to change, too." Dad went down the hall toward his bedroom. At first, Katy didn't understand what he meant. Then she looked down and smiled, realizing that she was still wearing the pink skirt and white blouse from the dress-up box. She rushed down to the basement, wanting to beat her dad outside. Katy stuffed the skirt and the blouse into the dress-up box, hurried back upstairs, put on her red tennis shoes, and got to the door, just before Dad came into the kitchen.

"I beat you!" Katy said with a smile. She went outside and got a basketball from the garage. Her dad followed.

"How about we play Pig?" Dad suggested.

"I forgot how," said Katy.

Her dad explained. "You take a shot. If you make it, I have to shoot from the same spot. If I make it, nothing happens. If I don't make it, I get a letter. The same if I make a shot. You shoot from the same spot and get a letter if you miss."

"Oh, I remember now," said Katy. "And the first one to spell 'pig' loses, right?"

"You got it," Dad said. Katy got a 'p' first. Then Dad got a 'p' and an 'i.' Katy was beginning to think that maybe she had a chance to win, but then her dad made a shot from a long way back. She realized that he had been playing easy.

"Daddy!" said Katy. "You know I can't make one from all the way back there!" Dad smiled and shrugged. Katy missed her shot.

The next shot that Katy made was close to the basket. Her dad would have to make one from the same spot. She stepped aside and passed the ball to her dad. He dribbled the ball, took aim, and shot. The ball went up, hit the backboard, and then the rim. As the ball rolled around the rim, Dad said, "Oh, come on!" as if saying it would really make a difference. The ball went in. Katy stamped her foot, folded her arms, and pretended to be mad. Dad went over to his daughter and tickled her.

"Okay! Okay!" she managed to say. Katy missed her next shot, but Dad made his. Katy went over and stood exactly where her dad had been. She shot the ball. It went around and around the rim.

"Oh, come on!" Katy said, trying her dad's technique. It didn't work for her, though. The ball went off the rim the wrong way and fell to the ground. Katy had spelled "pig" first. The ball began to roll down the driveway.

"You always win," said Katy, chasing after the ball.

"Aw, just wait a few years," Dad said with a smile. "I've had a lot more years to practice than you have!" Katy put the ball back in the garage and went inside with her dad.

When Dad said good night to his daughters that evening, he thanked Katy for playing basketball with him.

"You're welcome, Daddy," said Katy. She was glad that she had a father who would play basketball with her and then say thank you as if she had done him a favor. "Thank you," she said, hugging his neck.

It took Katy a long time to fall asleep. She was hot and her bug bites itched. It seemed that every time she scratched one, a different one would start to itch. Her hair was sweaty and she had a hard time getting comfortable, but she finally fell asleep. A few hours later, she woke up suddenly, shaking all over from a nightmare. She crept out of bed and into the hall. There were no lights on. She felt her way to her parents' bedroom door and knocked timidly. No one answered. Katy knocked again, a little louder.

"Come in," she heard her dad say. His voice sounded startled. Katy opened the door.

"What's wrong?" Mom asked.

"I had a bad dream," Katy told them, as she walked closer to their bed.

"Oh," said Mom compassionately. "Do you want to tell us about it?" Katy did. She climbed into her parents' bed and told them her dream.

"Anna and I were driving down our street," Katy began. "I know it sounds funny that we were driving, but it wasn't funny in the dream. All of a sudden, a great big tour bus came toward us. It took up the whole road. It started backing up to let us pass. Then I was outside and our van wasn't there anymore. Our street turned into the top of a huge cliff. The bus kept on slowly backing up and it got closer and closer to the edge of the cliff. I was just standing there, shaking my head, and quietly saying, "No, no," and then the bus fell off the cliff! I went over to the edge and watched it falling down, down, down. It was a really long way to the bottom. And then I felt like it was my fault because I should have waved my arms and screamed at the top of my voice so the bus wouldn't fall, but I hadn't. Then I found out that only the bus driver and his son were still alive after it fell and it was just awful and I got so scared!" Katy nestled close to her mom. Mom put her arms around her daughter and Dad patted Katy's back.

"It's going to be okay," Mom said soothingly. "It was just a dream."

"Let's pray," said Dad. "Father, I pray that You will comfort Katy and help her go back to sleep without any more bad dreams. Thank You for our precious daughter. In Jesus' name, Amen." There was a long pause and the three of them lay still in the darkness.

"You know what?" Katy whispered. "While you were praying, I smiled. Know why? It's because I felt like God was hugging me." Mom kissed Katy's head.

"That must have been a nice feeling," she whispered, and gave Katy a hug. "And now I think you need to go back to your bed and go to sleep. Okay?"

"Okay," said Katy. "Good night. I love you."

"I love you, too, Katy," Dad replied.

"I love you, Precious," said Mom. Katy climbed out of their bed and felt her way to her bedroom. She crawled into her own bed and held Sugar Plum tight.

"Good night, Sugar Plum," she said. "I love you. I love You, too, God. Thanks for the hug."

6

Being Different

Anna and Katy woke up the next morning when they heard their dad call them for breakfast. They hurried out of bed and skipped down the hall, arm in arm, to the dining room. Their parents and Seth were already at the table. Anna took her place beside Mom on one side of the table; Katy took her place beside Seth on the other. Dad sat at the head of the table. The five of them clasped hands and bowed their heads. Dad prayed for the Lord's blessing on their breakfast and their day.

When the cereal was eaten, Mom told the children that the dishwasher needed to be unloaded. Katy's heart sank as she looked out the window, longing to be out in the sunshine. At least they all three had to do it together.

They carried their bowls and juice glasses into the

kitchen and laid them on the counter. Seth opened the dishwasher and proposed a new method for unloading the dishes. He would put away the plates, Katy would put away the utensils, and Anna would put away everything else.

"No way!" cried Anna. "That's not fair. It leaves me with all the hard things!"

"We'll help you after we finish our stuff," said Seth.

"No," Anna said decidedly. "Plastic things are the worst to put away because they stay wet, and—"

"Kids!" came Dad's voice from the dining room. He wasn't yelling, but he was firm. "Stop fighting about it and just do it."

"But, Dad!" Anna called back. "Seth is making me put away all the hard stuff!"

"Not all of it!" said Seth.

"That's enough," came Dad's firm voice again. "No more arguing. Just put up the dishes." Seth and Anna looked at each other. Seth shrugged, obviously feeling bad since he had started it all by his suggestion. Katy was glad she had just been on the sidelines. They put the dishes away without another word.

When the dishes were unloaded, Seth and Katy went

outside to climb the maple tree in the front yard. They had a contest to see who could climb the highest. Katy climbed until she was afraid to climb any higher. Seth climbed until he couldn't climb any higher.

"Why can you always climb higher than I can?" Katy asked, looking up at her big brother.

"I just can," said Seth. "It's okay, though. I'm bigger than you are."

"Seth," Katy asked, "what do you want to be when you grow up?" Seth was silent for a moment.

"Well," he finally answered, "I've thought about being a baseball player. Or maybe I'll become President. You never know."

"I want to work in a fabric store. I love the way they slide the scissors to cut the fabric instead of going snip-snip-snip-snip. Do you want to play capture the flag?"

"It's not much fun with just two people. Besides, I want to work on programming that computer game I started yesterday. The book has to go back to the library tomorrow."

Katy and Seth climbed back down the tree. Katy jumped down from the lowest branch with Seth still a few feet above her.

"Ha!" she said with a smile. "I beat you down! I guess that's one good thing about not being able to go the highest!"

"I guess so," said Seth. "Congratulations!" He headed toward the door. Katy followed and poked her head inside the kitchen. Her mom was loading the dishwasher while listening to an audio recording. Katy paused and listened to a snippet of it. She heard something about the state of the public schools these days and how homeschooling protects children from the evil influences of the world.

"Mom?" Katy asked. Her mom raised one finger, telling Katy to wait just a minute. When the speaker reached the end of his sentence, Mom paused the recording and turned to Katy. Katy asked if she could go next door and play with Chinway. Chinway and her family were from Nigeria. Chinway's father taught at the university. Mom said Katy could go, and before Katy had closed the door, the recording was back on.

"Mom must be really serious about this homeschooling thing," Katy thought, as she walked across the yard toward Chinway's house. She walked around the hedge that separated the Porters' yard from their neighbors' yard next door.

Katy found Chinway playing with her little brother James. They were throwing a big rubber ball back and forth. James dropped it almost every other time. Chinway invited Katy to join in and the three of them played Monkey in the Middle until James got tired of it and went inside. Chinway and Katy continued to toss the ball, but they soon grew tired of that, too.

They sat down in the grass to look for four-leaf clovers. Katy's fair skin was different from the dark brown color of Chinway's. "Chinway's skin is different from mine," Katy said to herself, "but I think it's beautiful. Homeschooling will make me a little different, too. Different in some ways, but I'll still be like other kids, too, won't I? Is it going to make me too different?" Katy and Chinway sat side by side in silence, intently searching the clover patch for one that was different.

"Guess what," said Katy, as the two continued to search.

"What?"

"My mom and dad are thinking about homeschooling us when school starts." Katy waited for Chinway to reply.

"What's that?"

"It's where you do school work in your house instead

of in a school," Katy told her, "and your mom and dad are your teachers."

"Hmm," said Chinway. "That sounds pretty neat, but does it really work?"

"Sure it does," Katy answered. "Lots of kids homeschool now. The public schools are in a pretty sorry state these days and homeschooling protects them from the evil influences of the world. Public schools are turning out too many children who are rebellious, disrespectful, and disobedient." Katy was quoting what she had heard on the recording.

Chinway didn't know how to reply, and Katy didn't have any more to say because she hadn't listened to more of the recording. The two searched on in silence.

"I found one!" said Chinway finally. She picked the four-leaf clover and handed it to Katy. "You can have it," she said. Katy thanked her and held it in one hand while she continued to search with the other. She hoped to find one to give Chinway, but the door opened behind them and Chinway's mom called her in to clean her room.

"Bye, Katy," said Chinway, heading to the door.

"Bye! And thanks for the clover," said Katy. Katy walked back to her own yard. She sat down in the swing that hung from the crabapple tree, still holding Chinway's gift. Before long, she heard the side door open.

"Katy," Anna called, "Mom says we have to fold the laundry." Katy jumped out of the swing and ran across the front yard to the side door. Mom was in the kitchen stirring lunch, which was bubbling on the stove. The recording was still playing. This time there were several voices discussing the pros and cons of homeschooling.

"Do we have to do the laundry now?" Katy whined. Mom paused the recording and looked at her youngest daughter.

"Katy," her mom replied, "there's no point in complaining about it. It has to be done and it's your chore with Anna and Seth, so just go on and do it. You'll put away the laundry by yourself since you complained about it." There was a silence. "Yes, ma'am?" said Mom.

"Yes, ma'am," Katy replied. She shuffled across the floor and knew her mom was waiting for something else. She turned back around and put her arms around her mom's waist. "I'm sorry I complained," she said.

"Thank you, Katy. I forgive you. Now just go on and get it over with. I bet you guys will have it done in no time."

Katy followed Anna downstairs to the den. Seth was putting in a movie for them to watch while they worked. Katy cheered up when she saw that it was *Hairylympics*, one of their favorite cartoons. They all sat down to tackle the four baskets of laundry as they watched the animated animals compete for gold, silver, and bronze. They all laughed at the ostrich racing down the track.

They finished the laundry before the movie was over, but they all stayed until the end. When it was over, Katy told the others that she had to put everything away by herself. It took Katy several trips up and down the stairs to get all the laundry in its rightful place.

When she finished, Katy went to the kitchen. "I'm sorry, Mom," she said again, looking down at the pattern of yellow squares and rectangles on the kitchen floor.

"I forgive you, Katy," Mom replied. It felt good to hear those words again. The recording her mom had been listening to was finished.

"I told Chinway that we might homeschool this fall," Katy told her mom. "She said that it sounded pretty neat. I told her that the public schools are in a pretty sorry state these days and that homeschooling protects children from the evil influences of the world. I told her that public schools are turning out too many children who are rebellious, disrespectful, and disobedient. That's what I heard on your recording, so that's what I thought I should say." Mom looked as though she was trying to hide a smile.

"Maybe you could think of something else to say next time," she said gently. "Something like, 'It would give us an opportunity to study at our own pace and learn about things we are interested in.'" Mom was quoting, too, but Katy didn't know that. "Doing what is right for us doesn't mean we can judge other people if they do something different. Chinway goes to public school, and she's not rebellious, disobedient, or disrespectful. Neither is Ruth. They're both sweet girls like you. I know you all make mistakes and disobey sometimes, but my point is you all have the right kind of heart. Many public school kids are sweet and wonderful, but Dad and I want to protect you from the bad influences that are out there. We want you to learn our values and not the values of the world. We don't want your hearts and minds to be full of worldly teachings, but full of Jesus."

"Do you think homeschooling will make me too different?" Katy asked.

"Different isn't always a bad thing," said Mom. "God doesn't want us just to follow the crowd and do what they are doing because it's popular. Being different can be a good thing. Jesus certainly didn't go along with the crowd. He was different. Many people in this city don't meet with a church, but we do. We're different in that way already, and that's a good difference. We're different because we don't go see the movies other people see and we don't watch bad shows on television. We don't say certain words because we believe they are wrong. We're already different because we follow Jesus."

Katy thought about what her mom said and knew that she was right. Being different was okay. It was even good.

"But," said Mom, "we haven't decided for sure. You might be going to public school this fall."

"I hope not," Katy said. Mom smiled.

"I hope not, too," she said. Katy stayed in the kitchen and helped her mom until lunchtime.

After lunch, Katy remembered that she hadn't made her bed that morning. Making up the bottom bunk was difficult, but Katy finally got the sheets and blanket smooth and her pillow in place. She put Sugar Plum on her pillow, after trying unsuccessfully to Velcro her dress back together. Katy reached into her pocket and pulled out the wilted four-leaf clover. She laid it on the dresser. As she did, she looked over toward the fish tank. She gasped. Her eyes widened and filled with tears.

"Mommy!" she yelled. "Come here quick! Wiggly Worm is upside down! I think he's—" Mom hurried into the room. "Look!" said Katy, with tears streaming down her face. "Wiggly Worm is dead!"

"Oh, Katy," Mom said sympathetically. "I'm sorry." She drew her daughter close to herself and stroked Katy's long hair. Mom sat down on Katy's bed and Katy curled up in her lap and cried.

After several moments, Mom whispered, "Is it okay if I go call Daddy?" Katy nodded. She climbed out of her mom's lap and stretched out on her bed, hugging Sugar Plum. Mom went out of the room and shut the door.

"Why did he have to die, Sugar Plum?" Katy said, looking into her doll's blue eyes. Sugar Plum just smiled back at Katy, but Katy felt that Sugar Plum understood everything. "I guess some people would think it's silly to cry over a fish, but I don't care." A few minutes later, Mom knocked lightly on the door.

"Come in," Katy said, her voice muffled by the pillow. Mom came in and told Katy that Dad was coming home early so they could go to the pet shop before it closed and get another fish. Katy was glad, but she knew she could never like any fish as much as she liked Wiggly Worm.

In a little less than an hour, Dad was home from the office. He put Wiggly Worm in a small plastic container and dug a little grave to bury him in the back yard beside the fence. When all was completed, everyone piled into the minivan and headed for the pet shop.

"Can I help you?" a clerk asked as they entered the store.

"We'd like a goldfish," Dad answered. The clerk led the Porters past the dog toys and bird food and expensive tropical fish to a tank at the back of the shop.

"Which one would you like?" the clerk asked. Katy looked up at her dad.

"Go on and pick one," said Dad gently. Katy shyly stepped forward and knelt down to examine the fish. At first, she didn't know whether to get a skinny one or a fat one. Then she decided that the fat ones were probably healthier. There were fat light orange ones and fat dark orange ones and fat ones of every shade of orange in between.

"That one!" Katy said at last, pointing to a fat, dark orange fish. The clerk stuck his little blue net into the water and caught a fish. "No, not that one," said Katy. "*That* one!" Again the clerk caught a fish, and again it was not the one that Katy wanted. After three more attempts, he caught one that pleased her, but even Katy wasn't sure if it was the fish she had first picked out. The clerk pulled out the fish and quickly put it in a plastic bag full of water. He tied a knot at the top and handed the bag to Katy. She carried it carefully to the van, cradling it in her arms.

"I named him Big O," Katy announced at supper that night. "O stands for orange because he's orange. His nickname is You Cutie." Everyone laughed, but Katy had not meant for her fish's name to be a joke.

"I'm sorry," said Mom, trying to keep a straight face. "Those are very nice names."

After supper, Katy got a piece of paper from the small white clipboard on the counter beside the phone in the kitchen. She pulled a pencil out of the jar next to it, but as usual the lead was broken. She searched for a pencil with a good point and went back to the dining room table. She drew a picture of Wiggly Worm and wrote about what had happened that day.

When the lights were out that night and Katy was in bed, she whispered to Sugar Plum, "Big O is a nice fish, but I still miss Wiggly Worm. I liked him best." Katy closed her eyes and the constant *whrrrrrrrrr* of the fish tank soon put her to sleep.

7

The Potluck

"Hurry up, Katy!" Dad called, standing at the back door. "We're late!"

Katy ran down the hall, through the kitchen, and out the door. She was wearing her favorite dress. Her mom had made it for her. The dress was pink with small wreaths of blue and white flowers printed all over it. Best of all, it had a small heart-shaped pocket in the front. Two dimes jingled in it as Katy headed to the van. The cloth hearts that dangled from the matching bow in her hair bobbed up and down as Katy ran. It was Sunday, and the Porters were going to meet with their church. Katy started to jump into the van, but stopped.

"Seth, isn't it my turn to sit in the back?" she asked. Katy, Anna, and Seth had assigned seats, which rotated every Sunday. Katy was sure it was her week to have the back seat all to herself.

"I thought it was my turn," said Seth.

"But I'm sure it's mine. Anna had it last week, and now it's my turn. You're supposed to be in the middle." Seth thought for a moment and realized Katy was right.

"Sorry," he said. "You'd think I could remember from one week to the next!" Seth got up and Katy took his place. Seth climbed over Anna, who was sitting by the door, to his seat beside her.

"Seth! You're on my toe!" Anna cried. Seth moved his foot. "Now you're on my dress!"

"Kids, just sit down," said Mom. Sunday mornings were often stressful in the Porter household, trying to get everyone ready and out the door on time. "Honey, I don't remember if I turned the stove off or not."

"It's off," Dad assured Mom as he got into the van. "I checked it twice. Do we have all the food?"

"Yes, Jack," Mom answered. Dad started the car and backed out of the driveway. The Sunday morning rush drifted away as Katy began thinking of all the good things everyone in the church brought to the potluck lunches—things that the Porters didn't usually buy like fried chicken and Oreos. All the food the Porters were taking was on the back seat.

"Katy," said Mom, "hand Seth the corn so it doesn't spill, and you keep the rest of the food from tipping over, okay?" Katy handed Seth the bowl of corn. He carefully lowered it to the floor between his feet. When Dad stopped at the first stop sign, the peanut butter cookies almost slid onto the floor. Katy caught them just in time.

"Hold on to what you've got," said Dad as he made a turn. Katy held on to everything as best she could. When the Porters pulled into the parking lot, Katy was thankful that nothing had spilled.

It was hard for Katy to sit through Bible class that morning, thinking about the potluck lunch. She had eaten three of her dad's homemade biscuits for breakfast, but her stomach was already growling. She knew she shouldn't be thinking about lunch during class, but even the lesson was about food. Hearing about Jesus turning two fish and five loaves of bread into enough food for five thousand people made Katy even more hungry.

Near the end of class, Katy's teacher, Miss Angela, led a prayer. "Dear God," Miss Angela began. Katy could hardly stand it any longer. She was so hungry.

She looked around at the other kids, wondering if they were as hungry as she was. She knew she should be concentrating on the prayer, so she closed her eyes and bowed her head like the rest of the class.

"In Jesus' name, Amen," finished Miss Angela. Josh raised his hand. "Yes, Josh?" Miss Angela said.

Josh pointed at Katy. "She wasn't closing her eyes during the prayer," he said. Katy felt her face turn red. She didn't want the teacher or any of the others to think she was a troublemaker.

"Josh, how do you know that her eyes were open if yours were closed?" Miss Angela asked.

"I just opened mine a little," Josh replied. "Hers were open all the way."

Miss Angela started to reply, but her sentence was cut off by the bell, telling everyone that class was over. Even though Katy was sorry she hadn't paid better attention to the prayer, she was thankful to hear the bell.

"One more hour before we eat," thought Katy, as she walked down the hall. "I don't know if I can stand it! I'm so hungry." Katy went into the auditorium and found Seth and Anna sitting near the front. Katy sat down beside Seth. Dad and Mom slipped in after the first song.

"Where were you?" Katy whispered.

"Just talking to someone," her mom whispered back.

"Turn in your songbooks to number 342," said Delmas, the song leader. "3-4-2. This is for you, Katy."

Katy looked up in surprise. She was shocked to hear her name coming from the stage in front of everyone! She looked down in her songbook at number 342. "Jesus is Coming Soon" she read at the top of the page. Katy felt her face turn red again. That was her favorite song, but she wondered how Delmas knew. When the song was over, Mom leaned over to Katy and whispered, "After class he asked me what your favorite song was, but I didn't know why!"

In the middle of the assembly, the collection plates were passed around. The church put in money to support missionaries, pay for the building, and things like that. As a wooden plate came down Katy's pew, she reached into her heart-shaped pocket and pulled out the two dimes. They clanked when she dropped them into the plate. She looked forward to the day when she was

older and had enough money to bring dollar bills to put in the collection plate because they wouldn't clank.

Katy's dad soon went up to the front. He was the preacher for their church. He began his sermon by telling a story.

"A few years ago, we were on a trip and drove by a field of cows. One of our children noticed that the cows were all standing in a group in the middle of the field and said, 'Look! A cow meeting!'" A murmur of laughter went through the audience. Several people turned to look at the Porters, wondering which child it was. "I tell this story to say," Dad continued, but Katy didn't even hear him. She was the one who had said that, and now the whole church was laughing at her! She buried her face in her hands and again felt it turn red. It seemed like everyone was trying to embarrass her today. First Josh, then Delmas, and now her own dad.

After the last "Amen" was said, the whole church made its way to the fellowship hall where they would eat the potluck lunch.

"It's finally time!" Katy said to herself. She stopped at the water fountain to get a drink before going into the kitchen. There were two water fountains beside each other in the hall. One was tall; one was short. Katy was glad that she was tall enough to drink out of the taller water fountain. It made her feel like one of the big kids. While she was getting a drink, she felt someone pull her hair. She turned around and saw Delmas, the song leader, looking away as if he didn't know what had happened. Katy knew better, though, and they smiled at each other.

Several of the ladies began to bustle about in the kitchen, getting salads out of the refrigerator, warming up casseroles in the oven, and setting out plates, cups, and silverware. Mom and Anna helped in the kitchen while Katy stood beside her friends, Whitney and Megan, waiting. While she stood with them, Mr. Battle walked by. As usual, he pinched Katy's cheek. Katy gave him an embarrassed smile and wondered why everyone seemed to be picking on her!

"What's that horrid smell?" asked Mrs. Lanford after a few minutes of preparation.

"Oh, I smell it, too!" said Mrs. Carr. Everyone continued to get the meal ready, but the smell grew worse. Many of the children were pinching their noses and crying, "Pee-ew!"

The potluck was almost ready; but with the stench in the air, the food didn't look very appetizing.

Katy watched Anna. She was standing near the stove, talking with her friend Jenny. She saw them wrinkle their noses and could tell they were talking about the smell. She watched them move toward the stove and open the oven door. They peeked in, slammed the door shut, and stared at each other with wide eyes. Katy thought maybe they had seen a burnt casserole.

"Mom!" she heard Anna call out in a loud whisper. "Mom, come here quick!" Mom went over to Anna.

"What's the matter, Dear?" Mom asked. Anna pointed at the oven. Mom opened the door and looked inside.

"Eww, yuck!" Mom cried. Katy went over to see what was so disgusting about a burnt casserole. When she looked inside the oven, her stomach felt like it did somersaults all the way down to the floor. She felt sick. There, in the bottom of the oven, lay a dead mouse, baking along with the casseroles.

As soon as the oven door had been opened, the smell filled the room even more. Mrs. Lanford and Mrs. Carr came over to see what the trouble was.

"Oh, it's a mouse!" Mrs. Carr cried.

"Oh, dear!" said Mrs. Lanford, turning away. Word quickly spread through the congregation about the little critter in the bottom of the oven.

Katy was disgusted and wanted to run out of the kitchen, but she didn't want to get embarrassed again. She turned away and went back over to where Whitney and Megan stood. They were both holding their noses and laughing. Katy held her nose, too, but she didn't feel like laughing.

Mr. Carr volunteered to remove the mouse. Using a paper plate and a spatula he managed to get the mouse out of the oven. He took it outside and tossed it into the field behind the building. He threw the paper plate and spatula in the dumpster outside. The doors and windows were all opened to try to get the horrid smell out of the building. It helped a little, but not much.

The potluck went on as planned, except for being a few minutes late. Katy ate salad and Oreos, but she was careful not to eat anything that had been warmed up in the oven. She even passed by the fried chicken without touching a drumstick.

8

A Play

"What's your favorite team?" Katy asked Seth one afternoon as they were looking at their baseball cards. Katy collected baseball cards because Seth collected them.

"My favorite is the Cubs," Seth answered.

"Mine is, too. What's your second favorite?"

"The White Sox."

"Mine, too." Katy flipped through the baseball card album which held her favorite cards. "Do you want to trade any?" she asked.

"Sure," Seth answered. "Who do you want?"

Katy looked through some of her brother's cards. She didn't really care about batting averages and that kind of thing, so she looked for someone who had an interesting name. When she found one, she asked Seth if he would trade it. "You can pick one of mine," she said, "as long as he doesn't have on a green uniform or one with stripes. Those are my favorite."

"Okay," said Seth, being a good sport. "How about this one?" He held up one of Katy's cards. The player's uniform was blue, so Katy agreed.

"It's a deal," said Katy, as they made the swap.

"Katy!" Mom called from the kitchen. "Clean up and come help us, please!"

"Yes, ma'am! I'll be right there!" Katy called back. She closed her album and put the rest of her cards back in her card boxes. She carried them into her room and tugged on her drawer under the bunk beds. It was always hard to open. Finally she got it far enough out to put her cards away, but then she had to push and shove to get the drawer back in. After it was in place, she went into the kitchen.

"Yes, Mom?"

"Honey, help your sister set the table," Mom told her. "The Evans should be here any minute."

Katy picked up the forks and knives that were lying on the counter and carried them into the dining room.

She set them around the table, forks on the left and knives on the right.

Dick and Kathleen Evans were some of the Porters' closest friends. They had two children. Jenny was the same age as Anna and they had been best friends since kindergarten. Rachel was three years younger than Katy. Katy felt like a big kid around Rachel. She was proud of the fact that it was she who had taught Rachel how to write her name in cursive. It made Katy feel very grown up.

When the doorbell rang, Dad went to the door to welcome their guests. The Evans filed into the small entryway. Mom greeted them from the kitchen.

"Supper will be ready soon," she said. "Go on in and have a seat in the living room. Katy, I need you a minute. Put up those dishes on the counter, please." Katy put the pot in the drawer under the stove and the plates in the cabinet. Mom handed Katy a bowl of steaming green beans to carry into the dining room.

When supper was over, the four girls headed down to the basement. "Let's do another play," Anna suggested. The girls loved to put on plays for their parents and Seth. Their last production was *Romeo and Juliet* on roller skates.

They decided to act out a fairy tale this time. The four of them worked on their play for nearly two hours. They got the costumes together and made up songs. They gathered props and set up chairs for the audience. They worked on their lines. At last it was time for their parents and Seth to come down. After everyone was seated, *The Princess and the Pea* began.

Katy played the role of the queen who was searching for a princess for her son, the prince, to marry. Anna played the part of the prince. Jenny played the part of the princess who arrived at the castle one stormy night, wet and cold, and looking like a peasant. To see if the girl was really a princess as she claimed, Katy had her

French maid, played by Rachel, pile up twenty quilts and twenty mattresses. Underneath all of these, Katy hid a tiny pea. Katy then recited a poem that she and Jenny had composed for the scene:

> *I've got a pea,*
> *I'll put it in her bed.*
> *This is the test*
> *If my son she shall wed.*
> *For if she can pass*
> *This itty-bitty test,*
> *It will prove*
> *That she is a princess.*
> *If when she awakes,*
> *Her skin's black and blue,*
> *Then we will know*
> *That she has been true.*

The next morning in the play, the princess arose from a terrible night's sleep. She had tossed and turned all night because of the lump in her bed. The queen was overjoyed. She knew immediately that the girl was a true princess, for only a princess would have been able to feel the pea. The princess married the prince and everyone lived happily ever after.

When the show was over, the cast bowed and the audience clapped.

That night, after Katy and Anna were in bed, Katy whispered, "Anna?"

"What?" came the sleepy reply.

"Are you awake?"

"No."

"Yes, you are! I want to ask you a question. Will you go to the Acorn Lady's house with me tomorrow? It's not as fun without you."

"I don't know," Anna answered. "I doubt they are ripe, anyway. I'm really tired, Katy. Please just go to sleep."

"But will you?" Katy asked again, pushing up on Anna's mattress with her feet. Katy knew that Anna didn't like it when she did that. Then Katy ran her toes across the wooden slats that held up Anna's mattress. *Thump-a-thump-a-thump-a-thump-a-thump.* Katy knew that Anna didn't like that, either. That's why she did it. She ran her feet back down the wooden slats. *Thump-a-thump-a-thump-a-thump-a-thump.*

"Stop it!" said Anna in a loud whisper. She was more awake now.

"Answer me," Katy whispered back. "Will you go with me tomorrow?"

"Yes," Anna answered. "Just kidding. I'm just kidding that I'm just kidding. I'm just kidding that I'm just kidding that I'm just kidding. I'm just kidding—" Katy pushed on Anna's mattress with her feet again. She couldn't stand when Anna did that!

"Stop!" Katy said, in a voice that was a combined whisper and yell.

"Well, you stop bugging me and pushing up on the mattress!" said Anna. Katy let the mattress down. "I don't know if I'll go, Katy," Anna finally said. "Let's just go to sleep." There was silence.

Katy didn't like it when Anna used that tone and tried to sound like a grown-up. She hugged Sugar Plum tighter and whispered very quietly, "You'd gather acorns with me if you could, wouldn't you, S.P.?" Katy made Sugar Plum nod her head. "I knew you would," she said. "I love you, Sugar Plum." Katy lay in her bed for several minutes, thinking.

"Anna?" she whispered at last.

"Yes?"

"I'm sorry. I shouldn't have bugged you or tried to make you mad."

"That's okay, Katy," Anna replied. "I'm sorry, too. Look, I don't think it will work to go to the Acorn Lady's house tomorrow. I'm supposed to go over to Jenny's. Maybe another time, okay?"

"Okay," Katy answered. "Good night, Anna. I love you."

"I love you, too, Katy."

Katy's eyes were heavy. She was nearly asleep when she heard the sound of rain. Suddenly she remembered that she had forgotten to pray.

"God," she prayed silently, "I'm really sorry I fought with Anna. Thank You for the Evans, especially Rachel. Please keep us safe tonight and . . . ." Katy didn't finish her prayer. She was sound asleep. She slept peacefully, but only for a short time.

9

Lightning

Katy woke up suddenly as her room was lit up by lighting. In one . . . two seconds she heard thunder. "That was close," she thought. Katy looked over at the clock by the fish tank on the dresser. It was 12:03 a.m. Katy reached for Sugar Plum to hug her, but she couldn't find the doll anywhere. In the blackness, Katy felt around under her blanket and then on top of it. She reached to the floor and brushed her hand across the carpet. She reached down behind the headboard. Another clap of thunder sounded outside. Katy was almost ready to scream and run to her parents' room. She put her hand down between the bed and the wall and gave a sigh of relief. She felt Sugar Plum's arm, pulled her up, and hugged her close.

The storm finally seemed to be passing. Katy was almost back to sleep when she heard a thunderous crackling boom. It was the loudest thunder she had ever heard in her life. Immediately, the smoke alarms went off and the smell of smoke spread through the house. Katy screamed, "The house is on fire!" She didn't know if this was true, but she thought it must be if the smoke alarms had gone off. They had only beeped for a moment, and now were silent. Katy jumped out of bed, still holding Sugar Plum. Anna climbed down the ladder, but Katy was already in the hall. Her Dad came out into the hall at the same time. Katy went to Seth's door and banged hard.

"The house is on fire!" she yelled. Dad and Mom began to look around the house. They didn't see any smoke or fire. Dad ran downstairs to check for fire but didn't find anything. Katy was scared they were all going to die. "We have to get out of this house," she kept saying, over and over.

"Jack, maybe something's burning in the attic," Mom said in an anxious tone.

"I'll check. Seth, go get the ladder from the garage so I can check the attic through the entrance in the living room. I'll go on and look in the entrance in the girls' room. We'll have to check both, since you can't see from one part to the other up there." Seth walked slowly toward the garage, still half-asleep.

"Girls," Mom said to Anna and Katy, "go get the old photo albums and put them in the van, just in case." Anna and Katy hurriedly obeyed. Dad went into the girls' playhouse and climbed up into the attic. He didn't see anything.

Mom went to the cordless phone in the kitchen to call 9-1-1; but when she picked it up, there was no dial tone. Thankfully the corded phone in the basement still worked. Even though everything seemed to be okay, the Porters wanted someone to come check their house, just to be sure.

Seth soon came back in the house, but without the ladder. Dad asked him where it was.

"You said to put it in the van," Seth answered.

Dad laughed, which sounded good at a time like that. "No, I didn't! Mom told the girls to put the albums in the van! I need the ladder to check the attic! Seth, think. Why would I be concerned about rescuing that old ladder? Just imagine telling someone, 'Our house burned down, but we saved the ladder!'" Everyone laughed. Seth went to get the ladder. Anna and Katy piled the albums on the back seat of the van. Dad and Seth checked the attic from the living room entrance. Everything looked okay.

The lightning had stopped, but the rain continued. Mom was still on the phone. She was having trouble getting through to the fire department. Katy was still scared. She kept saying, "We have to get out of this house. We have to get out of this house."

"Katy," said Mom, "God is taking care of us. I don't think our house is on fire. If it was we would all be outside. I am just calling to—Hello?" Mom had finally gotten through to the fire department. She told them what had happened, and they promised to be right over. Everyone waited.

The firemen weren't "right over" after all, but at last the Porters saw flashing lights coming toward their house. They looked out the window and saw a police car pull up in their driveway.

"Why are the police here?" Anna asked. A police officer got out of his car and came to the door. Mom told him what had happened.

"Well, I'll look around until the fire department gets here," the officer told them. "We're having trouble getting calls through because of the storm." The police officer walked around outside with a flashlight. Mom closed the door.

"What if our house was going up in flames?" she said fretfully. "If the calls can't get through in a storm, they need to get better equipment."

The Porters continued to wait. The cuckoo clock ticked and tocked. Soon after the little bird came out to tell them that it was 12:30, the Porters saw a fire truck coming down their street. It pulled into their driveway and two men got out. Then came another fire truck. It parked on the street. A third one followed.

"Three of them?" said Seth. "I don't think it's quite that bad!" The firemen looked around the house and assured the Porters that everything was safe. "There's a tree next door that was struck by lightning," one of the firemen explained. "Probably what happened is the electricity from the lightning went through the trunk and out the roots, touching the underground wires. In doing so, it sent an electric charge into your house. It looks like you're safe, though."

The police car and fire trucks soon drove away. The Porters began going through the house checking their electrical appliances. One of the firemen had told them that the lightning might have damaged some of them. He was right. Dad's old record player wouldn't turn on. The phone in the kitchen didn't work. The garage door remote didn't work, either. The switch plate behind the light switch in the hall had broken and was lying on the floor in pieces. When the lightning hit, it sent an electrical current through the wires so strong that it blew the switch plate off the wall. Several of their electrical appliances did not work, but it could have been much worse.

The Porters made a circle in their living room, and Dad said a prayer. He thanked the Lord that they were all safe and that there hadn't been a fire.

"And now," said Dad, looking at his children, "I have a lecture. I don't want you to have the wrong idea. If our house ever catches on fire, you get out. You don't worry about dolls or photo albums or ladders or anything. You get out. Tonight was different. There was no fire. The alarms went off, but only briefly. We smelled something funny, but didn't see smoke anywhere. Do you understand the difference?" Seth, Anna, and Katy all said they did.

Katy lay down on the couch in the living room. She was still too scared to go back to her bed. Before she fell asleep, she remembered what she had prayed earlier before the lightning hit.

"God," she whispered, "I know You heard me ask You to keep us safe, because You did. Thank you."

Just before she fell asleep, Katy heard the bird in the cuckoo clock come out to tell the Porters it was two o'clock. It had been a long night.

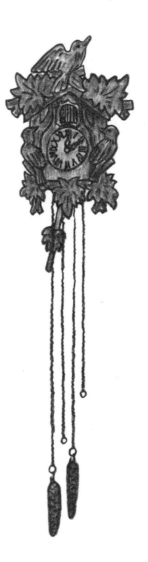

10

The Basement

One Sunday afternoon, the Porters went to the church building a few hours before the evening assembly. Dad had a meeting, and Mom had some work to do for her Bible class. Seth and Anna went to the church library to read; but Katy and Megan decided to go exploring. Megan Carter's parents were out of town, so Megan was spending the day with the Porters. Even though they had been in the church building countless times, the thought of exploring sounded fun. They thought maybe there was a hidden place somewhere they hadn't yet discovered.

After receiving Mom's permission to explore outside, the two girls walked around the building, looking for something new and interesting. The large field behind the church building was bright yellow, covered with dandelions. Katy and Megan picked dozens of the little flowers, which turned their hands a nasty, sticky yellow. With dandelions in hand, they walked through the field to the far side. Here the land rose slightly and the low, grassy hill was surrounded by trees.

"Did you know we might be homeschooling this fall?" Katy asked her friend.

"Really? Why?"

Katy thought before she spoke. She remembered the conversation with her mom in the kitchen and wanted to be sure she didn't say anything that would hurt Megan's feelings. "My mom and dad are thinking that maybe it's

best for us," Katy began. "Things didn't go well in school last year, and they're thinking maybe it would be better for us to be at home. They haven't decided for sure yet."

"Do you want to?" Megan asked.

"Yes," Katy answered. "I really do."

There was a pause before Megan asked, "What do you want to do now?"

"We could play that we're running away from an orphanage," Katy suggested.

"No," answered Megan, "we always play that. How about a race? I'll race you to the birch tree beside the front door."

Katy and Megan stood side by side, and Katy said, "Go!" They raced across the lawn as fast as they could. Megan reached the birch tree three paces ahead of Katy. They both sat down to rest, panting. Katy soon suggested that they go inside to cool off.

"Okay," Megan answered, "but what will we do in there? There's nowhere new to explore."

Katy's eyes suddenly lit up. "Hey," she exclaimed, "did you know that there's a basement in there? I've only been down there once, but it's real neat! The ceiling is so low that even I have to bend over to walk."

"A basement?" said Megan. "I didn't know that! Show me!" She was excited now, too. The girls left their dandelions under the birch tree and Katy led the way inside. Katy stopped by the teacher's workroom to make sure it was okay with her mom.

"That should be fine, but be careful down there," said Mom.

"Yes, ma'am," said Katy, "we will."

Megan and Katy stopped at the water fountain at the end of the hall to rinse the yellow stickiness from the dandelions off their hands. Katy led Megan on to a secluded hall in the back of the building and down a short flight of stairs. Katy showed her the door into the basement. It was a small door, about a foot off the floor, and only two feet tall. Katy took hold of the two silver knobs that stuck out from the door, turned them both to the left, and pulled. The tiny door creaked open. Megan and Katy looked at each other and smiled. They scrunched down and stepped into the darkness. Katy found the light switch and flipped it on. The dirty basement was lit by a single light bulb that hung from the ceiling. Megan pulled the little door shut behind them.

"I didn't even know this was here," Megan whispered. "This is so cool!" The basement was the kind of place that made you whisper without even thinking about it. "But it's a little spooky," she added.

"Yeah," Katy answered, also whispering, "but this is nothing compared to over there!" She pointed to an opening which led into pitch blackness. There wasn't a light bulb in that part of the basement. The two girls looked at each other. They both wanted to go into the darkness, but they were both afraid.

"Come on!" Megan finally said. "We might as well." The girls walked through the opening into the darkness. They walked across the floor, each holding tightly the other's sweaty hand.

Katy tried to figure out what was on the floor above them. "I think it's my dad's office," she concluded.

The girls tried to walk to the opposite side of the dark room, but the ductwork blocked their way. They decided to turn back. They were relieved to step back into the lighted part of the basement.

Megan looked at her watch. "People will be coming for church soon," she said. "Let's go out before they get here so no one will see us come out of our secret place."

Katy went to the door. "Okay," she said. "I'll hold it open, and you go out first, but before that we have to make sure no one is out there. Once we're sure, you go and then I'll follow. We have to go fast, though, so no one will see us. That would spoil things. Ready? One, two, three!" Katy pushed on the door. It didn't budge. "Oh, no!" she cried out in a frightened whisper. "The knobs are only on the outside! Megan, we're trapped!" Megan's face turned white.

Katy began to tremble slightly. She knocked on the door. "Hello?" she called hoarsely. She knew she would have to call loudly if anyone was going to hear her, but somehow her voice didn't do what she wanted it to. She cleared her throat and called again, louder this time. "Can anyone hear me?" No one answered. Katy and Megan slowly turned toward each other. They were both scared, but the moment their eyes met, they burst out laughing.

"What are we going to do?" Megan said at last. "I mean, how are we going to get out of here?"

"I don't know," Katy answered. "We could go to the part of the basement that's under the auditorium and make people think there are mice down here! Then they would want to come set some mouse traps and maybe they would find us before we starve to death."

"Yeah, and then we could go crawl in the oven!" Megan said, laughing. Katy didn't understand what her friend meant at first, but then she remembered the little visitor in the oven at the last potluck.

"That's gross!" Katy said, but she couldn't help laughing.

After their laughter died away, Megan sat down on the dirty floor. She rested her chin in her hands. Katy was just about to join Megan when they heard footsteps on the stairs above them. Katy and Megan began banging on the door.

"Hey!" they called out. "Down here!" They heard the footsteps stop, then descend the stairs and come toward the little door.

"Who's in there?" said a man's voice. Katy and Megan turned pale again. They were scared of who might be on the other side of the door. "I said, 'Who's in there?'" the voice repeated.

"Um, just us," Katy managed to answer. "If you turn the silver knobs at the same time and pull, we can get out." Megan and Katy heard the man fumbling with the knobs. They looked at each other nervously. Slowly the door opened. The girls' faces turned bright red. There was Delmas, the song leader! No one knew exactly what to say. Finally Delmas broke the silence.

"Hello," he said. "Fancy meeting you here."

"Hi," Katy answered. She climbed out and Megan followed. "We didn't know there weren't knobs on the other side."

"I see," said Delmas. As Katy walked by him, Delmas gave her hair a gentle tug. Katy turned around and smiled, and Delmas looked up at the ceiling.

"Yes?" he said, as if he didn't know why Katy was looking at him. "What?"

"Thanks for rescuing us," said Katy.

"Glad to be of service," Delmas replied with a smile.

Megan and Katy hurried to the auditorium. Most of the people had already sat down and the service was just about to start. Megan's parents were not getting back into town until late, so Megan sat with the Porters. During the second song, the girls' eyes met and they both broke out into a fit of giggling. Mom, who was sitting on the other side of Katy, looked at them and put her finger to her lips. "Shh," she said.

Megan and Katy avoided looking at each other all through the sermon because they knew if their eyes met again, the giggles would come right back.

11

Tennessee

Early one Monday morning, Dad came into Anna and Katy's room to wake them up. "Girls," he said, "time to get up. We need to leave in about half an hour." The Porters were going to Tennessee to visit their relatives.

Katy did not want to open her eyes. They had all been out late the night before, and she was sleepy. Anna climbed down from the top bunk and pulled off Katy's cover. Katy moaned. "Come on, Katy," said Anna. "We don't have long!" Katy slowly sat up in bed and put her feet on the floor. She wanted to plop back down, but she forced herself to get up anyway. Katy hugged Sugar Plum.

"Bye, S.P. Be good while I'm gone," she whispered. Katy quickly made up her bed and got dressed. She picked up her suitcase and the bag of things to do in the car that she had packed the night before. "Bye, Big O," she said as she passed the fish tank on her way out of the room. She looked to make sure the automatic feeder was still in place in the bottom of the tank. "It will let out enough food for you two every day," Katy told the fish, "so don't worry about us not being here to feed you."

The last minute preparations were finally finished and the Porters piled into the van with all their luggage. It was about an hour later than they had planned to leave, but that was to be expected. Before the brown minivan pulled out of the driveway, Dad prayed for a safe trip.

It was a long drive to Tennessee. Katy reached in her bag and pulled out a coloring book and some crayons. It was hard to stay in the lines while riding down the interstate, though, and sometimes coloring in the van made Katy feel sick. After one picture, she put her coloring book and crayons back in her bag. She pulled out two toy horses and two brushes.

"Do you want to brush one?" she asked Anna. Anna chose the pink horse with blue hair and Katy handed her one of the brushes. Katy began brushing the hair of the purple horse whose mane and tail were pink. Anna and Katy brushed the horses' hair until it gleamed. They braided the long manes and tails and tied ribbons at the ends.

"Look, Mom," Katy said. "Don't they look pretty?" They held their horses up and Mom turned around and admired them.

"Very nice," she said with a smile. Katy placed the horses in the window next to her seat. She hoped that the passengers in the cars that passed by would notice them. Katy liked to look at the passengers in other cars and try to imagine where they were going.

After lunch, Seth, Anna, and Katy played Car Tally. Anna made a chart with ten different car colors on it. Seth and Katy called out the colors of the cars they passed. "Red . . . black . . . white . . . white . . . red . . . blue . . . green . . . white . . . black . . . ." Anna tallied the colors on the chart as the others called them out. When the time was up, Anna counted the tally marks and announced the winners.

"Ahem. Ladies and gentlemen, I will now announce the winning colors of the National Car Tally Game. Third place goes to black. Let's give it up for the blacks!" Seth and Katy applauded. "Second place goes to red. Three cheers for red! Hip, hip, hooray! Hip, hip, hooray! Hip, hip, hooray! And now, the winner of the National Car Tally Game is . . . drum roll, please." Katy beat her hands on the arm rest as if it were a drum. "The winner is . . . white!" Anna and Katy cheered with great enthusiasm. Everyone clapped, even Mom, and Dad tapped one hand on the steering wheel. After their car tally game was over, Seth fell asleep and Anna started reading. Katy passed the time by singing "There's a Hole in the Bucket." By the time they reached Tennessee she had sung it twenty-one times. Most of the time she sang under her breath so she wouldn't drive everyone crazy.

"Are we in Tennessee yet?" Katy asked her dad after every few rounds of the song. Sometimes he said, "We're getting there," sometimes he said, "Not quite yet," and sometimes he simply said, "Nope." Finally, though, he announced that they were in Tennessee. Dad stopped at a gas station just across the state line. While he pumped the gas, Katy and her mom went inside to pick out a snack for everyone.

Katy saw postcards at the checkout and asked if she could buy some. When Mom said she could, Katy picked out four different scenes.

"This one is for Whitney," Katy said, holding up a picture of three horses with hills and a barn. The word "Tennessee" was written across the top in fancy letters. "She sent me a postcard when they went to Florida last year, so I want to send her one, too. The others are for Rachel, Megan, and Ruth."

When they were back on the road, Mom handed out the snacks. Before long the Porters were driving down the old familiar street in the little town of Ashland City where Mom had grown up. Grandmother and Granddaddy came outside the moment the brown minivan drove up. Everyone exchanged hugs.

"How's my little Stink Pot?" Granddaddy asked Katy, giving her a big hug.

"Good," Katy answered. She liked it when Granddaddy called her Stink Pot.

"Supper's almost ready," Grandmother told them, "It'll be just a few more minutes." Grandmother and Mom went inside to finish supper. The rest of them carried in the luggage.

They all soon gathered around the table for spaghetti and meatballs. Katy got to sit on the old green metal stool to eat. After supper, the Porter children went outside to the creek. The creek was only two or three feet wide and just a few inches deep, but they didn't have anything like it near their house in Illinois. Seth suggested they build a bridge as they had on their last visit. The bridge, made of sticks and rocks, turned out better than the last one they had built.

"We can actually walk across this one!" said Katy, as she tried it out.

Granddaddy came outside to join them just as it was getting dark. "You little monkeys want to go down to Stratton's for a cone o' cream?" he asked. Their faces lit up. They were all delighted to accept the invitation!

Stratton's was one of only a few restaurants in the whole town. It was like a 1950s diner. The waitresses wore poodle skirts that Grandmother had made. She was a seamstress who did sewing and alterations for people in the town. The walls of the restaurant were lined with old Coke signs, pictures, and all sorts of advertisements from many years ago. A black and white photograph of a boys' baseball team hung in one corner. In it, if you looked closely, you could see Katy's Uncle Steve when he was a little boy. The restaurant had a jukebox, too. Sometimes Katy picked songs for it to play.

The restaurant had booths and tables, but Katy's favorite place to sit was on a spinning stool at the counter. She was glad to see that there were four empty stools in a row. They all sat down.

"Evening, Charles," a waitress said to Granddaddy. Everyone at Stratton's knew Granddaddy well because he spent so much time there drinking coffee with his friends. "These your grandkids?"

"Yep. Them they are and these are them," Granddaddy said. He had a funny way of mixing up words and saying things the wrong way on purpose.

The waitress smiled. "Coffee?" she asked Granddaddy.

Granddaddy nodded. "Yeah, and get me a vanilla cone, too." The waitress looked at the children and asked what they wanted. Seth ordered a chocolate ice cream cone. Anna and Katy each ordered a vanilla ice cream cone dipped in chocolate, called a brown derby.

The brown derbies were good, but messy! The hard chocolate coating cracked in a few places and the ice cream dribbled down Katy's chin and onto the counter and her clothes. One drip ran down her hand and made it all the way to her elbow before she could stop it.

When they had finished, the owner said, "Bye, Charles," as the four of them left the restaurant.

"See ya," Granddaddy called back. When they got back to the house, Grandmother was sewing. Her sewing machine was in the kitchen. Mom was sitting at the table talking with her. Katy asked for permission to make something. Mom suggested poodle skirts for Katy's dolls. Grandmother got some turquoise fabric scraps and silver fabric paint. Katy sat beside her mom at the table and Mom cut out two circles. She painted one and Katy painted the other. Katy laid them in the living room to dry.

That night, Dad and Mom slept in the bedroom that had been Mom's before she went to college. Seth slept on the couch in the living room and Anna and Katy shared an inflatable mattress on the floor beside him.

When Katy woke up the next morning, she could hear voices in the kitchen. Mom soon came into the living room and sang the Porter family's "getting up song."

"The bright sun comes up," sang Mom, "the dew goes away. Good morning, good morning, the little birds say." Mom tickled Katy's feet. "Get up girls and boy," she said. "We're going to go see Mama Sue and Daddy Leland in a little while." Mama Sue and Daddy Leland were Katy's great-grandparents who also lived in Ashland City.

Seth, Anna, and Katy got up and got ready. They sat down at the kitchen table for breakfast. The grown-ups had already eaten. Katy sat on the side of the table that was in front of the window. An air conditioner sat in the window behind her, blowing cold air right against her back. It was loud and blew her hair in her face, but the coolness felt good. Grandmother brought over three brown plastic bowls and three spoons. The milk and cereal were already on the table. Katy, Anna, and Seth each poured themselves a bowl.

"Do you want any toast?" Grandmother asked.

"Yes, please," said Anna loudly, trying to be heard over the noise of the air conditioner.

"And me, please," Katy said.

"No thanks," said Seth, pouring himself another

bowl of cereal. Grandmother opened the bag of bread, pulled out two slices, and placed them in the toaster. While the bread was toasting, she poured three glasses of apple juice. She brought them to the table on a tray, along with the butter and toast.

"You ready, Stink Pot?" Granddaddy said, walking into the kitchen a few minutes later.

"Almost," said Katy as she gulped down the last of her apple juice. After the table was cleared, the Porters and Grandmother and Granddaddy all squeezed into the van. The drive to Mama Sue and Daddy Leland's house was on a curvy, hilly road. Katy, Seth, and Anna, scrunched into the back seat, pretended they were on a roller coaster.

At their great-grandparents' house, Anna and Katy played store in the living room with some old containers that Mama Sue kept in the hall closet. Seth played on the piano, and the grown-ups sat in the dining room and talked. After they had been there about an hour, Mama Sue got up and went into the kitchen.

"I've got some peanut butter fudge in here and a little bit of chess pie," she called. No matter what time of day it was when they visited Mama Sue, she always wanted to feed them as much as they would eat. Everyone crowded into the kitchen. Katy couldn't wait to taste the peanut butter fudge. "Mama Sue must make the best fudge in the world," Katy thought to herself. "It's perfect."

Some sat around the table, but there weren't enough chairs for everyone. Katy went to get the pink stool from beside the washing machine. She brought it to the table and sat down beside Granddaddy. The stool was pink because that was Mama Sue's favorite color. Katy liked to find all the things she could in Mama Sue's house that were pink. Besides the stool, the kitchen table was white with a pink border, and the kitchen counters were pink. The dishpan in the sink was pink, and Mama Sue's fancy dishes were pink, too. The walls in the dining room were painted pale pink, and there was a pink couch in front of the pink and white curtains. Part of the house even had pink carpet, and in the bathroom everything was pink—a pink tub, a pink toilet, pink tile, pink sinks, a pink trash can, pink towels, pink curtains on the window, a pink shower curtain, and pink designs on the wallpaper. There was even a cover for an extra roll of toilet paper on the back of the toilet, and it was pink! Mama Sue liked pink. Katy noticed that Mama Sue was wearing a pink shirt. She looked under the table and even her socks were pink!

It was soon time for goodbye hugs to go around. Katy hugged Mama Sue and Daddy Leland. Before they left, Daddy Leland said to Katy, "You're prettier than a speckled pup." Katy smiled shyly and told her Daddy Leland that she loved him.

The Porter children played in the basement of their grandparents' house that afternoon. They discovered new treasures among their mom's and uncle's old toys and clothes. They found an old wheelchair and played darts with the dartboard Seth dug out from a pile of boxes.

Uncle Steve, Aunt Betsy, and their baby daughter Ashley came over for supper that evening. After supper, Katy watched Aunt Betsy prepare Ashley's bottle. Katy desperately wanted to give Ashley her bottle, but she was too embarrassed to ask if she could. She went over to Mom and whispered in her ear, "Will you ask if I can give Ashley her bottle, please?"

"You can ask," Mom answered. Katy looked at Aunt Betsy and wondered if it was worth asking, or if she should just give up the idea of feeding Ashley.

Aunt Betsy caught on and said, "Do you want to give Ashley her bottle, Katy?" Katy nodded. "If Ashley doesn't mind, I don't mind," said Aunt Betsy. "You just go on in the living room, and I'll bring her to you."

Katy went into the living room and sat in the big brown rocking chair. It was the same rocking chair she remembered Granny, Grandmother's mother, rocking in before she died.

Aunt Betsy came in and laid Ashley in Katy's arms. Ashley cried at first, but as soon as Katy gave her the bottle, she quieted down. Katy put a small pillow under Ashley's head and rested it on the wooden arm of the rocking chair. After Ashley started drinking her bottle, the pillow slipped out and Ashley's head went *bonk* on the arm of the chair. Ashley screamed. Katy was horrified. She didn't know what to do, but Aunt Betsy soon walked in from the kitchen. She picked Ashley up out of Katy's lap and continued giving Ashley her bottle herself. Aunt Betsy assured Katy that everything was fine. Ashley soon stopped crying. Katy could feel a tear run down her cheek. She went into the back bedroom and cried just a little. When she came back out, Aunt Betsy could tell that she had been crying.

"I'm really sorry," Katy said meekly.

"Oh, that's all right!" Aunt Betsy said. "She's done with her bottle, but would you like to hold her?" Katy was relieved to know that she wasn't going to be hated for the rest of her life. She sat on the couch this time, and Aunt Betsy put Ashley onto her lap. Katy grinned from ear to ear when Ashley fell asleep while she was holding her.

On Wednesday, it was time to say goodbye. Katy told her grandparents she loved them and thanked Grandmother for letting her make the doll skirts. She gave them each a hug and climbed into the van. The Porters drove away, waving as they went.

12

Columbia

The drive from Ashland City to Columbia wasn't very long. The Porters arrived in the middle of the afternoon. They drove by the house where Dad grew up, and he showed them again the field where he used to play baseball with the other children in the neighborhood.

Katy wondered what her Dad's mother was like. She was from England and had died before Katy was born. Granddaddy Wes met her during World War II when he was in the army and stationed in Bristol, England. Sometimes Anna and Katy liked to talk with a British accent just for fun. Granddaddy Wes got married again a few years after his first wife died.

When the Porters pulled into the driveway of the red brick house where Katy's grandparents lived,

Granddaddy Wes and Mema came outside to meet them.

The Porters stepped out of the van and followed Granddaddy Wes and Mema into the den. The grown-ups started talking while Anna sat and listened. Seth and Katy wanted to do something else.

They were allowed to play with any of the games on the shelves behind the sliding door in the den. Seth opened the door and pulled out Parcheesi. Katy followed him out of the den and into the living room. The two of them sat down on the rose-printed carpet to play. It didn't take Seth long to win.

Mema soon came in to tell them they could help themselves to a drink, if they wanted one. Seth and Katy went into the kitchen to crush some ice in the ice crusher which was mounted to the cabinet above the sink. Anna was already there, getting the ice tray out of the freezer.

Katy put a stool in front of the ice crusher so they could reach it. Seth and Katy let Anna go first. Anna got up on the stool and put four ice cubes in the top of the crusher. She held the lid down with her left hand while turning the crank with her right. The ice came out in little chunks into the red cup screwed onto the crusher. When Anna had crushed eight pieces of ice, she unscrewed the red cup, poured the crushed ice into a glass, and screwed the red cup back on. Seth crushed his ice next, but he didn't need the stool. When Katy's turn came she pulled the stool back in place and crushed her ice.

They went out into the garage where Mema kept the soft drinks. They were a special treat since the Porters rarely had soft drinks at home.

When their glasses were empty, Katy and Anna went outside. They went though a door in the kitchen onto a screened-in back porch. Katy pulled the small, red wooden see-saw out from under the bench beside the door. The see-saw rested on two rounded pieces of wood like the rockers of a rocking chair. Katy stood on one end, and Anna stood on the other. The wood made a thud on the concrete each time one of them went down as the other went up.

Anna slid the see-saw back under the bench before they opened the screen door of the porch and stepped out onto the mossy stone patio in the back yard. Ivy grew up a short wall and up the side of their grandparents' house. Anna and Katy sat down across from each other at the iron table on the patio. They pretended they were rich girls wearing long, lacy gowns and sipping tea from china teacups.

The Porters went with Granddaddy Wes and Mema to their church that night for a Bible study. After they got home, Anna and Katy went back to the bedroom where they always slept and tried to think of something to play. They lay down side by side on the big bed and thought.

"School?" Anna suggested.

"No, not school. How about olden days?" Katy said.

"We don't have any of our dress-up clothes," Anna replied. "It would be boring."

"Okay," said Katy, "then how about orphanage?"

Anna thought a moment. "Okay. Why don't you be an orphan and I'll be the mean matron?"

"My name will be Emma," said Katy. "What's yours?"

"Gertrude Hazelworth," Anna decided.

The game began. Gertrude Hazelworth was always telling Emma and the other imaginary orphans to clean the floors and wash the dishes and make the beds and dust the cobwebs. She was always getting mad if something wasn't done just right.

"Emma, I want you to take down the curtains and wash them," Matron Hazelworth said in a mean, raspy voice.

"But we washed them yesterday!" Emma replied innocently.

"Don't talk back to me! I'll teach you not to do that again!" Anna pretended to push Katy onto the bed, but really Katy just fell back onto it. "Take *that*! And *that*! And *that*!" Anna said in her Gertrude Hazelworth voice while pretending to punch Katy's nose. On the fifth "And *that*," Anna accidentally didn't pretend. She really punched Katy's nose! Anna was horrified.

"Katy!" she said, no longer being Matron Hazelworth. "I'm so sorry! I didn't mean to! Are you okay?" Katy held her hands over her nose and nodded, but tears were forming in her eyes.

"Let me see if it's bleeding," Anna said. Katy put her

hands down and Anna looked. "I don't see any blood." Katy got up and walked into the den. She went over to Mom and climbed into her lap.

"What happened?" Mom whispered.

"Anna punched me," Katy replied. Anna was standing in the doorway.

"I didn't mean to," she mouthed across the room. "I'm sorry."

"I know," Mom mouthed back. Katy lay her head on Mom's shoulder. Mom stroked Katy's hair. Before she knew it, Katy had fallen fast asleep.

The next morning Katy sat down at the kitchen table to write her postcards. She wrote to Whitney first.

Dear Whitney,

I am having fun visiting our family in Tennessee. I got to hold my baby cousin Ashley, but I accidentally bumped her head on the rocking chair. We built a bridge across the creek that goes by my grandparents' house. Have you been playing any baseball lately? I bet you'll make all-stars again this year. See you soon!

Your friend,
Katy

When she had written all four cards, Granddaddy Wes gave Katy four postcard stamps. Katy took the cards out to the mailbox and put the flag up.

On Thursday night, the night before they were going to leave, Granddaddy Wes and Mema took the Porters out to eat at a restaurant called Catfish Campus. When Granddaddy Wes saw someone he used to work with at the local newspaper office, Katy had to smile and be introduced. It always made her feel funny, but she had learned to smile anyway. Everyone had ice cream after supper, which was Katy's favorite part. She pulled the lever and watched the ice cream, half chocolate and half vanilla, swirl out of the machine into her bowl.

On the way back to Granddaddy Wes and Mema's house, Dad told Seth, Anna, and Katy that they needed to get ready for bed right after they got back to the house so they could get an early start in the morning. Katy wanted to whine and beg to play just a little bit more on the Nintendo since they didn't have one at home, but she thought better of it.

After they were ready for bed and their suitcases were packed up, Seth pulled out the hide-a-bed from the couch and Anna and Katy went to their bedroom.

They lay in bed and looked up at the gold bubbles on the light fixture by the moonlight coming in from the big windows on either side of the bed until they fell asleep.

The next morning the Porters left only thirty minutes behind schedule. Granddaddy Wes and Mema gave each of the children a package of six mini boxes of cereal to eat on the road.

"Goodbye, Mema," Katy said, giving her a hug. "Bye, Granddaddy Wes."

13

Cousins

Mom was in the driver's seat as the Porters headed toward the city of Chattanooga to see Dad's brother and his family. Rain began to fall as they drove out of Columbia. The windshield wipers squeaked back and forth, going faster as the rain fell harder. Finally, the rain let up and the sun began to shine.

"Look in front of us!" Mom exclaimed suddenly. "There's a rainbow!" Everyone in the back bent and twisted, trying to see out the front window. "Cool!" said Katy. "You can really see all the colors." As they drove on, the rainbow continued to arch in front of them. It was as if they were chasing it down the highway.

"God's world is truly amazing," said Mom. They continued to follow the rainbow as it gradually faded away until, as they neared Uncle Alan and Aunt Shirley's house, it vanished completely.

After lunch, Aunt Shirley decided to take Katy, Anna, and their cousin Brittany on an outing. Brittany was two years younger than Katy. Bradley, Brittany's older brother, was one year older than Katy. He stayed at the house to play with Seth.

Anna and Katy sat on either side of Brittany in the back seat. Aunt Shirley parked the car in a parking lot near a pedestrian bridge which crossed the Tennessee River. They all got out and headed across. Katy looked down at the boats and barges floating down the river. She was glad the rain had stopped.

When they reached the other side, Aunt Shirley led the girls to the carousel, which was housed in a white building with large windows all around and a blue roof. They stood in line to buy their tickets. While they waited, Katy examined the animals and picked out the one she wanted to ride. She hoped no one else was wanting the same one.

The carousel glittered with gold and the animals were painted bright colors. Aunt Shirley paid for the tickets, and the four of them walked through the gate.

Katy headed straight for the animal she had picked, a frog wearing a yellow jacket and khaki pants. Katy climbed on his back while Brittany climbed onto the white horse in front of her. Anna chose to ride a rabbit and Aunt Shirley sat in a sleigh on the outer ring of the carousel. The music began, the animals went up and down, and the carousel turned. Katy held on to the pole and looked up, watching the gears move the frog up and down. When the song was over, the carousel slowed to a stop and Katy climbed down. They had to hurry out the gate before the next people came in to take their turn on the carousel.

They walked back into the hot summer afternoon and Aunt Shirley suggested they go to an ice cream shop for a treat, which sounded good to everyone. They walked into the shop and Aunt Shirley told them they could pick any flavor they wanted. Anna decided on mint chocolate chip right away. The clerk scooped out a generous serving, put it in a waffle cone, and handed it to Anna.

Brittany chose rainbow sherbet. Her tongue and lips had already turned green before Katy had made up her mind about which flavor to have. It often took Katy a long time to make up her mind. She walked from one end of the counter to the other, examining the buckets of ice cream and trying to decide. When a big group of loud teenagers walked in, Aunt Shirley suggested that Katy hurry and decide before the group got to the counter. Katy told the clerk she would like one scoop of cookies and cream. Katy began to lick the delicious treat as they walked out of the shop. She was satisfied with her choice.

It was almost time for supper when they got back to Uncle Alan and Aunt Shirley's house. While Aunt Shirley and Mom prepared the meal, Anna and Katy went upstairs with Brittany to her room. Brittany opened the window and they all three sat on the bed, wondering what to do until supper.

"We could do a concert," Anna suggested. Brittany wanted to know who the audience would be. "The whole world!" Anna replied. "We can sing out the window!"

They gathered at the open window and began to sing out, loud and strong.

There was a farmer, had a dog
And Bingo was his name - O!
B-I-N-G-O, B-I-N-G-O, B-I-N-G-O
And Bingo was his name - O!

"Row, Row, Row Your Boat" as a round didn't turn out very well. By the end of the third round they were all laughing and singing the same words together, instead of one after another as they had begun. They kept singing until they were called down for supper.

"Beautiful concert, girls," said Mom, smiling, as everyone was sitting down at the dining room table.

The three cousins laughed. "It was Anna's idea!" Brittany said. Anna shrugged, embarrassed, and looked down at the mashed potatoes Aunt Shirley had just served her.

The Porters left the next morning to begin the long drive back to Urbana, Illinois. When they reached home, the first thing Katy did after Dad unlocked the door was run into her room and give Sugar Plum a hug.

"Did you miss me?" Katy asked her doll. Sugar Plum's

blue eyes stared back. "I knew you would. I missed you, too! Hello, Big O!" Katy waved at the fish tank from her bed. Katy closed her eyes and prayed, "God, thanks for bringing us back home safely. I love You, Father. Thank You for loving me."

When they were both in bed, Katy whispered to her sister, "Hey, Anna? Will you go to the Acorn Lady's with me tomorrow?"

"What's your fascination with that place?" Anna replied. "Why do you want to go there so badly?"

"I just do," Katy replied. "Will you?"

"We'll see," said Anna. Katy sighed. Anna had recently started using that grown-up phrase, "We'll see." Katy knew that it meant no, but she decided not to bug her sister any more.

"I guess Mom and Dad will be deciding about school pretty soon," Anna said. "I wonder what they'll decide."

"I hope we do homeschool," Katy answered. "Do you?"

"I don't know," said Anna. "In some ways yes and in some ways no." They were both tired from the long trip, and soon fell asleep.

14

Under the Bed

The following Monday afternoon, Katy walked into the kitchen where her mom was talking on the phone. Anna was standing at the sink getting a drink of water.

"We would love to," Katy heard her mom say. "No, don't worry about the short notice! We don't mind. Can I bring anything?"

Katy walked over to Anna and whispered, "Who's she talking to?"

"I can't tell for sure," Anna answered. They both fell silent to listen for more clues.

"Yes, we had such a nice time," Mom was saying. "We got to see my little niece again. We saw her at Christmas, but they change so fast at that age! Well, I'd better go.

We'll see you tonight. What time should we come? Six o'clock sounds great. All right, we'll see you then. Bye." Mom hung up the phone.

"Who was that?" Anna and Katy asked at the same time.

"It was Ella Carter," their mom answered. "She invited us over for supper tonight." Anna and Katy were delighted. Mom told them that they were to bring dessert. Anna had already unpacked her bags from their trip to Tennessee, so she received permission to stay in the kitchen and help make the dessert. Katy wanted to help, too.

"You will have to get your things put away," Mom told Katy, "before you can do anything else."

"Yes, ma'am," said Katy, as she hurried to her room. "We get to go to Megan's tonight, Big O," Katy said to her fish, "but right now I have to get unpacked, so you just swim around and watch me." Katy unpacked her clothes first, putting the extra socks back in her dresser drawer, hanging up the clean clothes, and throwing the dirty clothes down the laundry chute in the bathroom. The laundry chute took the clothes to the basement where the washing machine was. When Katy had put away the coloring book, crayons, toy horses, and all the other things she had taken on the trip, she joined Anna and her mom in the kitchen.

"May I help?" Katy asked. The brownies were almost finished, but Mom let Katy stir in the chocolate chips and help Anna press them in the pan. The brownies smelled delicious as they baked in the oven.

It was Anna's week to sit in the back seat of the van. Seth and Katy shared the middle seat as Mom drove to the church building to pick up Dad from work.

Dad wasn't quite ready to go when they reached the church building. He had a lot of catching up to do after being in Tennessee for a week. Mom went inside to do a few things for her Bible class. While they waited in the van, Seth, Anna, and Katy talked about all they wanted to do with Colin and Megan.

Several minutes passed. The three sat in silence, waiting for their dad and mom. They waved to the secretary when she left and hoped their parents would soon follow. The minutes dragged on and the children wondered what was taking so long. They were becoming impatient. Finally the glass front door opened and Dad came out, holding his briefcase and a stack of papers. He stood there, holding the door open with his foot, waiting for Mom to turn the lights off in the hall and foyer. Dad reached into his pocket to pull out his keys. When he did, the stack of papers slid out from under his arm. The wind picked them up and began scattering them across the parking lot. Seth, Anna, and Katy jumped out of the van and ran after the flying papers. When they had all been retrieved, they carried them back over to their parents who were standing beside the van.

"Why didn't you let me lock the door, Jack? I had a key right in my hand," Mom was saying.

"I didn't think of that, Eva," Dad answered shortly. Katy looked at Anna and then at Seth. Seth and Anna looked at each other. They knew the tone of voice their parents were using. Katy felt a terrible tightness inside her when her parents used that tone. She didn't like it when they argued.

"Don't just stand there, kids, go on and get in the van," Dad told them. They handed their dad the papers they had gathered. Anna climbed in first and sat in the back seat. Seth and Katy followed. Dad closed the door after them. Dad and Mom stood outside talking for a few more minutes. Katy wanted to cry, but she knew her eyes would still be red by the time they got to Megan's house if she did, so she held the tears back. When Dad and Mom got into the van, no one said anything.

When the Porters pulled into the driveway of the Carters' house, Megan came outside to meet them. All of the Porters smiled, but Katy could see that her parents' smiles were strained and a little unnatural. She wondered if Megan could tell. Katy knew that everybody had arguments sometimes, but she didn't like it when her parents did.

Megan led the Porters inside. Mom joined Mrs. Carter in the kitchen and Dad sat down in an armchair across from Mr. Carter in the living room. Seth and Colin sat down at the computer in one corner of the living room to play a pinball game while Anna and Katy followed Megan to the den. Katy didn't feel like laughing and having a good time when she knew her parents were upset, but she decided to try.

"Mom said supper's almost ready," said Megan, "so we don't really have time to start a game or anything." Katy suggested they listen to some records on Megan's old record player. When Megan put on the record about a policeman directing traffic, one of their favorites, Katy almost forgot her parents' argument in the parking lot as they all laughed and sang along. They had listened to the song countless times. After Megan started the song for the third time, Mr. Carter called them for supper.

At the table, Megan sat between Katy and Anna and Seth and Colin sat beside each other on the opposite side. After Mr. Carter said the prayer, he began serving the roast beef. Katy saw that her mom was smiling her usual smile. When Mr. Carter made a joke, Katy noticed that her dad laughed for real and not just to be polite.

"Maybe they're not upset anymore," Katy thought, and she hoped she was right.

When it was time for dessert, Mom served the brownies while Mrs. Carter scooped out generous servings of ice cream for each one.

"These are delicious, Eva," Mr. Carter said after his first bite.

"Thank you," said Mom, "but I can't take all the credit. Anna and Katy helped." Anna and Katy looked at each other and smiled.

Seth and Colin finished their supper first and asked to be excused. Colin wanted to show Seth a new computer game. When everyone else had finished eating and the table had been cleared, Anna, Katy, and Megan stood in the kitchen listening to their moms talk. Soon Megan asked Anna and Katy if they wanted to go upstairs.

"Sure," Katy answered. "Let me check with Mom and make sure it's okay." Katy tapped on her mom's shoulder and waited a little impatiently for Mom to turn around. When she did, Katy whispered in her mom's ear, "Is it okay if Anna and I go play upstairs with Megan?"

"Yes," Mom whispered back, "but remember the rule about leaving the door open."

"Yes, ma'am," Katy answered. She and Anna and Megan tried to think of something to play as they walked upstairs to Megan's room.

"Let's do something different tonight," said Anna, "something besides the usual poor girls or princesses or school. I have an idea! How about I am a famous newscaster and you two are my daughters. How does that sound?" Megan and Katy thought it certainly sounded different, but fun just the same. Megan would be the big sister who had to take care of Katy, who was just a baby, since their mother had died the year before.

"You'd better hurry, Dad, or you'll be late for the newscast!" said Megan, beginning the game. Anna picked up Megan's "Going to Grandma's" suitcase, pretending it was a briefcase, and opened an imaginary door.

"Good bye, Darlings," said Anna, in a deep voice. They all giggled. "Don't forget to watch the news."

"We won't," said Katy, trying to sound like a baby. In a few minutes, Megan looked at the clock on the wall and saw that it was time for the news. Anna picked up an empty picture frame and held it up to her face, pretending it was the television screen.

"Good evening," said Anna, in a deep voice. Megan and Katy couldn't help but laugh. "I'm Don Ruther. This just in. Two cheetahs are said to have escaped from the San Diego Zoo and are on the loose. Please, ladies and gentlemen, if you see a cheetah run past your house tonight, don't open the door to take a picture and don't yell out the window to your neighbor. Call the zoo immediately. This is of the utmost importance. They are counting on you. If you see the cheetahs, call 1-800-ANIMALS. Don't delay, call today." By this time, Megan and Katy were flat on their backs on the bed, laughing. When they were able to control themselves, they sat up and Anna continued with the newscast.

"In other news today, the National Association of Gigglers will be holding their annual breakfast tomorrow morning at 8:27 a.m. at the circus tents on West Bazooka Street. Bonkers the clown will be making a special appearance. And now this." Here, Anna proceeded to perform a series of commercials. "Do you think you can't have chocolate ice cream for dessert? Well, yes you can! Introducing the all-new, fat-free, calorie-free, sugar-free, everything-free chocolate ice cream bars from DIETS brand ice cream. Only twenty dollars per box! Each box contains one ice cream bar."

For the next commercial, Anna imitated a Scottish man playing bagpipes. She sang,

Scotland, Scotland, Scotland away,
I, I want to be in Scotland today.
Scotland, Scotland, Scotland away,
I, I want to be in Scotland today.

"Call ScotsAir today for great rates to Scotland from anywhere in the continental U.S., except where you are. We now return to the news with Don Ruther." Megan got up and pressed the frame Anna was holding to turn off the television.

"It's time for you to go to bed now, Little Molly." Megan put a blanket over Katy and put a teddy bear in her arms. "Good night, Molly."

"Gaa-gaa, Goo!" said Katy.

The three girls pretended it was the next day, and Megan and Anna took Katy to have her portrait made. Katy made all sorts of funny poses and Anna made the clicking sounds of the camera. They pretended to look at all the pictures on a computer screen.

"That's my favorite," Anna said, pointing to a pretend picture.

"We could hang that one in the living room," said Megan. "And this one would look good in our bedroom, and that one in the bathroom."

"In the bathroom!" the girls heard a muffled voice from under Megan's bed say. "Who would hang a fancy portrait in the bathroom?"

"Colin!" Anna, Katy, and Megan exclaimed at the same time. They all got down on the floor and looked under the bed. Sure enough, there was Colin. He had been under the bed throughout their whole game.

"I thought you were playing the computer with Seth!" said Megan, appalled at what Colin had done.

"I was," said Colin, "but while you three were in the kitchen after we ate, I just thought I'd come up here." Colin scooted out from under the bed and dashed out of the room. Anna, Katy, and Megan were horrified that Colin had heard their game, but as soon as he was out of earshot, none of them could hold back their laughter any longer.

It was late when the Porters got back in the car to drive home. When they had pulled out of the Carters' driveway, Dad spoke.

"Kids," he said, "I need to apologize about earlier." Katy had been so engrossed in their newscaster game that she had forgotten about the disagreement in the parking lot. "I didn't treat your mother well, and I'm sorry. I was wrong."

"I'm sorry, too," Mom added.

"We forgive you," said Anna.

"Sure," Seth added. Katy looked out the window and up at the street lights. Sometimes it was hard for her to say the words she knew she needed to say. As she sat silently, she thought about how many times she had to say, "I'm sorry," and how good it felt when someone else said, "I forgive you."

"I forgive you, too," Katy said. She felt better when she said it, and she knew her parents did, too. Katy pressed her face against the window and looked up at the sky. She said a silent prayer and thanked God for her family.

Katy slept late the following morning. When she woke up, Anna's bed was already made. Katy walked down the hall, still wearing her pajamas. The house was quiet. She found Anna reading in the living room but didn't disturb her. She walked downstairs where Seth was playing marbles. Katy found her mom sewing in the den.

"Good morning, Sleepy-Head," said Mom, giving Katy a hug.

"Good morning," Katy answered with a yawn. She watched her mom carefully sew a hem on the tablecloth she was making. When her mom seemed to have reached a good stopping place, Katy asked if they could make something together.

"I think we could manage that," said Mom. "Why don't you look through my fabric scraps and see what you can find." Katy looked through her mom's scraps. She saw white and thought of making a bunny; she saw green and thought of a turtle. She thought about using some of the blue to make a dolphin, but she decided on a piece of brown fabric instead.

"How about an owl out of this?" she asked her mom, holding up the fabric. "We could use buttons for eyes, and here's a piece of yellow felt we can use for a beak and feet."

"That sounds good. Those scraps are from the curtains I made to go in our old house," said Mom. She laid aside the project she was working on and made room for Katy's owl on the table. Mom drew the outline of an owl on the brown fabric. Katy cut it out carefully with her mom's fabric scissors. While Mom sewed the front and back of the owl together, Katy looked through the bag of buttons to find some that looked like eyes. She picked out two bright blue buttons.

When the front and back of Mr. Owl were sewn together, Katy began to stuff him with fluffy white stuffing while Mom cut a beak and two feet out of the yellow felt.

As Mom glued the beak and feet on the owl, Katy decided to ask the question that had been on the tip of her tongue for the last several minutes. "Mom, you're not mad at Dad anymore are you?"

"No, Katy," Mom said gently. "I'm sorry we had an argument last night. I was wrong to get on to Dad for not letting me lock the door."

"But Dad said he was the one who was wrong," Katy said.

"We both were, Katy. Usually when you and Anna or you and Seth have an argument, you're both at fault, right?" Katy nodded. "Well, sometimes Daddy and I both do something wrong and we get upset with each other and we have an argument."

"But do you still love each other anyway?" Katy asked.

"Of course we do, Katy. Your dad and I love each other very much. We always will. Don't you worry about that, okay?" Katy smiled and nodded. She knew her mom was telling the truth.

When the owl was finished, Mom went back to her tablecloth. Katy watched the needle go up and down as her mom hemmed up the last side.

"You can get yourself some cereal if you want some breakfast," Mom said.

"Okay. I am getting pretty hungry," said Katy. She started to leave the den, but turned back and gave her mom a hug. "I love you, Mom. Thanks for helping me make the owl."

"You're welcome, Katy," said Mom. "I love you, too." She gave Katy a kiss on the forehead.

That night in bed, Katy held Sugar Plum in one arm and Mr. Owl in the other. "God," she prayed, "thanks for the fun time I had at Megan's. And thanks that my mom and dad love each other and that they love me, too. And thank You for Mr. Owl and that Mom made him with me. In Jesus name, Amen."

15

Croquet and 7-Up

The following morning was bright and clear. Katy had an urge to go for a bike ride. She asked Seth if he would ride with her. If it was okay with their mom, they would ride down to the school parking lot near their house, which was always empty this time of year.

"Sure you can go," Mom said. "You'll need to be back by eleven o'clock, though. Irene just called and wants you two and Anna to come over a little later." Seth and Katy were delighted by this news and assured their mom they would be home in plenty of time. They headed outside to get their bikes from the garage.

"Bye, Mom!" Seth and Katy called as they rode their bikes down the driveway. Mom waved to them through the open kitchen window. They pedaled down the strect.

Seth was in front. Katy had to pedal hard to keep up with her brother.

They reached the parking lot a few blocks away. It was completely empty. Since they had the whole lot to themselves, Katy and Seth rode in big circles and long zigzag patterns. They made huge figure eights and rode along the painted lines marking the parking spaces. Seth suggested they mark out courses and time each other to see who could ride through them first. Seth marked one out and Katy was first to ride through it. She began on the side of the parking lot next to the building and rode all the way to the other side. Then she had to turn around, ride up and down ten rows of white lines and stop on the handicapped symbol on the space near the door of the school.

"One minute, eleven seconds," said Seth. "Nice job! Now it's my turn." He handed his watch to Katy and rode to the starting position. When Katy said, "Go," Seth pedaled hard. By the time he reached the handicapped symbol, only fifty-seven seconds had passed.

"You win," Katy announced, rather reluctantly. "Congratulations." It was her turn to mark out the course and this time Seth would go through it first. Katy's course went all the way around the parking lot beside the grass, then zigzagged across the lot three times. It ended under the awning at the front doors of the building. Seth completed the course in one minute, thirty-two seconds. Katy was determined to beat him. She rode to the starting point and waited for the signal from Seth. He raised his arm in the air and Katy tightened her grip on the handlebars. As soon as his arm went down, Katy was off. She peddled hard all the way around the lot. She did her three zigzags across the lot and finally screeched to a stop under the awning. Seth was there waiting with his watch.

"One minute, twenty-nine seconds," he said with a smile. "You won fair and square by three seconds." Katy beamed. She was delighted, for once, to be the victor. Breathless, Katy stood by her bike while Seth rode leisurely around the lot one more time. He joined her again under the awning and suggested they head home. Seth led the way back down their street and up the driveway. They parked their bikes and went inside for a glass of water.

At eleven o'clock, Mom drove Seth, Anna, and Katy to Irene's house. Irene had befriended the three children soon after the Porters moved to Illinois when Katy was just a toddler. She was like a grandmother to them. She wouldn't let them call her "Mrs. Andrews" or "Miss Irene," but had always been just "Irene," the dear lady who loved them and was their special friend.

After Mom dropped them off, Irene decided that they would play croquet before they went to lunch. Seth got the croquet set out of the garage and they went to the back yard to set it up. Irene's yard boasted the delightful smell of roses. The beautiful flowers were in bloom all around the familiar red house. While Anna and Katy tightened the handles of the wooden mallets, Irene hammered the two stakes into the ground, one on each end of the yard. Seth set up the white wickets in a figure-eight pattern between the stakes. The wickets were made of metal, and when stuck in the ground they looked like small gates for the balls to pass through. The winner of the game would be the first to get their ball to go through all the wickets on the right side of the yard to the stake at the opposite end, then through the wickets on the left, back to the starting stake.

Irene said they would go in order from youngest to oldest, so Katy stepped up beside the stake and laid

her green ball in place. She aimed her mallet and hit
the ball. It went through the first wicket, but hit the side
of the second and bounced back. Since she had made
it through one wicket she received a second shot. She
took aim, but again the ball hit the side of the wicket and
stayed there without going through.

Anna was able to hit her blue ball through the first
two wickets in one shot, but even her two bonus shots
didn't take her through the third. On Seth's first turn,
he got his red ball through the first three wickets. Right
away, Irene's yellow ball caught up with his.

The game progressed with Irene and Seth battling for first place, Anna comfortably in third, and Katy trailing far behind. Irene and Seth were hitting their balls back down the second side long before Katy had made it down the first. The game began youngest to oldest and ended exactly opposite, with Irene coming in first, Seth in second, Anna in third, and Katy trying desperately just to make it back to the starting stake to achieve fourth place.

After the croquet set was put away, it was time for lunch. Irene took the children to a pizza restaurant called The Jolly Roger. The Porters didn't eat out very often, which made this excursion even more special.

When they got back to Irene's house, they played a card game called 7-Up. Irene pulled a deck of cards and some poker chips out of a drawer. Seth got a card table and three folding chairs from a closet off the living room. Anna set up the table in front of the couch where Irene sat. The children sat in the folding chairs on the other three sides of the table. Irene shuffled and dealt the cards while Katy divided up the poker chips. Seth won the first hand of the game; but in the end, Anna was victorious, having the most poker chips of all.

Hide the Thimble came next. Katy got to hide the thimble first. Irene, Seth, and Anna went into the den and waited while Katy looked around the living room for the perfect spot. She started to hide the thimble under the couch, but then thought of the plant on the table in front of the window. Katy put the thimble on her forefinger and then pressed it into the dirt. She pulled out her finger, leaving the thimble behind, almost buried in the dirt. She went to the den door.

"Ready!" she announced. The others came in and began to search. They looked all over the room while Katy gave out clues.

"Seth is the hottest," she said. "Now Anna's hottest. Irene is getting warm. Seth is freezing! Anna is getting warmer, but now colder. Irene is hot! She's burning up! She's on fire!" Irene looked all around the flower pot and even inside it, but she didn't see the thimble. Seth and Anna came over to where she was.

"I found it!" Anna called, pulling the thimble out of the dirt.

"Oh," said Irene laughing, "and it was right under my nose that whole time!" Katy laughed, too.

After five more rounds of Hide the Thimble, Seth

pulled the Star Reporter game out of the closet in the bedroom at the end of the hall. It was an old board game that Irene's children had played when they were little. Irene left Seth, Anna, and Katy to play this game by themselves. She went to her recliner beside the front window and sat down with the newspaper. The children set up the board and embarked on a race to collect the most points by visiting different locations on the map to gather stories for a newspaper.

When they were finished, Anna put Star Reporter back in the closet. She came back to the living room with a bingo game called Musingo. Seth went into the den to play the piano while Anna and Katy played Musingo. They took turns winding the plastic organ grinder who played music and showed which spaces to cover on the boards. Katy was the first to cover up five spaces in a row with the small tokens. "Musingo!" she called out.

After the second game was over, Irene put down her newspaper and got up. "If you will put away the table and chairs," she told them, "and put the game back in the closet, I'll get the ice cream out of the freezer and we can have some before your dad comes."

"Thank you!" they all replied. Seth folded up the

table and chairs and put them in the closet while Anna and Katy put all the game pieces back in the box and put the game away.

They all went out onto the front porch with Irene, who handed them each an ice cream popsicle in the shape of Mickey Mouse. Irene ate one, too. The chocolate coating and vanilla ice cream tasted good. A quick, warm breeze blew by and set the wooden whirligigs, which hung from the roof at the edge of the porch, spinning wildly. When everyone was finished, Irene collected the wrappers and sticks in the cardboard box from which the popsicles had come. She set the box beside the front door.

Irene and Anna sat in the two wooden chairs, painted red to match the house. Katy and Seth sat on the edge of the stone planter which went across the length of the front porch while they all waited for Dad to arrive.

When it was time to leave, the children all thanked Irene and piled into the minivan.

"Thanks for having them, Irene. I know they enjoyed it," said Dad.

"It was my pleasure, Jack," Irene replied.

As they drove away, they watched Irene wave and then walk back up onto her porch and pick up the cardboard popsicle box. Katy loved Irene. Irene had been all alone since her husband died. Her children lived far away. Katy had heard Irene and her mom talk about health problems that Irene had dealt with. Katy didn't understand what the problems were, but she knew they must have been unpleasant. Katy knew that Irene loved the Lord. She saw her at church three times every week. She knew that Irene picked up two women who couldn't drive anymore and brought them to church with her every Sunday morning.

Katy looked back at the red house with the big trees in the front yard. She looked at the front door through which she had walked many times and behind which lived a wonderful lady. Katy leaned her elbow on the armrest and placed her chin in her hand. "Dear God," she prayed silently as she looked out the window, "please make me like Irene some day."

16

The Patch

Summer was almost over. Katy had been to five swimming lessons over the summer, and this was the day of the final one. All of the students who passed the class would get a patch with a red seahorse on it. Katy couldn't wait to receive her patch. For the past few weeks she had been imagining where she would ask her mom to sew it. She thought about having it on her backpack, a shirt, or a blanket. She imagined the patch sewn on a beautiful piece of cloth, framed, and hanging on the wall over the fish tank. She thought a seahorse near Big O and Incognito would make the goldfish feel more at home. Wherever the patch ended up, Katy couldn't wait until she had it.

Katy's teacher had told them that this week they

would get to jump off the diving board. Katy was nervous about that. "Come on," she told herself, "it's not that deep. Miss Jenna will be down there to catch you, anyway! You're the oldest girl in the class. You have to get that patch!" No matter how much she tried to encourage herself, Katy was still nervous.

The last lesson was a review of what Miss Jenna had taught during all the other lessons. Katy wasn't the best swimmer, but she tried hard.

"Everyone follow me," Miss Jenna told all the girls near the end of their lesson.

"This is it," Katy thought.

"We're going to walk down to the diving board and you will all stand in line by the ladder. I'll be in the water to catch you when you jump off."

Katy and the six other girls, all of whom were beginners in swimming, lined up behind Miss Jenna. Katy was the fourth girl in line. They walked along the edge of the pool, down to the deep end, to the low diving board. As she stood in line with the other girls, Katy looked up at the high diving board. She watched the big kids jump off and do flips in the air.

"If they can do that," she thought, "I can do this,

right? I'm just going to jump. I don't have to do all those fancy dives and flips."

The first girl in line, Alexi, walked out to the edge of the diving board. She looked down at the water and started to cry.

"Come on, Alexi," Miss Jenna coaxed. "It's not that far. I'm right here. I won't let you go under." Alexi continued to cry. Then she turned around and walked back. She sat on the edge of the pool and cried some more.

"It must be really far down," Katy thought. "I thought Alexi was brave."

The second girl, Holly, climbed up the ladder. She was the best swimmer in the class. Holly walked to the edge of the diving board and jumped into the water. Miss Jenna caught her without letting her head go under water. Katy breathed a sigh of relief. Holly had done it. Katy would do it, too.

Now it was Brooke's turn. She climbed the ladder, walked to the edge of the board, and looked down. Miss Jenna came back from helping Holly to the side of the pool. Katy could tell that Brooke was scared. After hesitating a few seconds, Brooke jumped off the board into Miss Jenna's arms. Miss Jenna helped her to the side of the pool. Katy trembled slightly. "I'm probably going to be like Alexi," she thought. "I'm going to get up there and start crying."

"Come on, Katy," she heard Miss Jenna call. "Your turn."

Katy stepped onto the diving board and walked across it taking tiny steps. She reached the end and looked down. Miss Jenna was right there to catch her, just like she had been for Holly and Brooke.

Miss Jenna looked up, shielding her eyes from the sun overhead. "Come on, Katy," she said.

Katy was scared. She had never jumped off a diving board before. She bent down to scratch her leg. It didn't really itch, but it delayed her jump that much. She bit her bottom lip and looked into the water. She was almost ready to turn around and give up, but then she thought how nice a red seahorse patch would look hanging above Big O or proudly displayed on her backpack. "Okay," she said aloud. "One . . . two . . . three!" Katy leaped off the diving board. What happened next was all a flutter in her mind as she slipped through Miss Jenna's arms and down into the water. Katy began beating her arms and kicking her legs trying to get back to the surface. Miss Jenna quickly reached down and pulled Katy up. Katy sputtered and coughed. She rubbed her eyes.

"Oh, Katy!" Miss Jenna exclaimed. "I'm so sorry! Are you okay?" Katy nodded. Miss Jenna helped her over to the edge of the pool and Katy climbed out and sat next to Brooke. "Are you sure you're okay?" Miss Jenna asked again. Again, Katy nodded. Miss Jenna swam back to the diving board and the next three girls jumped off, one after the other. Last of all, Alexi walked to the edge of the board.

"I think I can do it now," Katy heard her say. "I just didn't want to be first." Alexi jumped off and Miss Jenna caught her.

"We all did it," Katy said to herself. "Now we can all get a patch, I'm sure. I was afraid that Alexi might not get one if she didn't jump, but now we can all get one!"

The last swimming lesson was over. Miss Jenna walked her class to the offices near the bathhouse. She went inside one of the offices and came out holding a stack of patches. She handed one to Holly. She handed one to Brooke, and one to Alexi. She handed a patch to each of the other three girls, and then she came to Katy.

Katy's smile faded away when she saw that Miss Jenna's hands were empty.

"You forgot me," Katy said timidly.

"Well, Katy," Miss Jenna began, "maybe you can get a red seahorse next summer. You just didn't quite do as well as you could have. Now, this doesn't have anything to do with the diving board thing. That was my fault. It was the other lessons that you didn't quite pass." Miss Jenna paused. "Wait here just a minute. Let me get you something." Miss Jenna turned back to the other girls, "You can go now, girls. I've enjoyed having you in my class. I hope to see you next summer!" Miss Jenna walked back into the office. Katy stood in stunned silence. She hoped with all her heart that Miss Jenna was going in to get her a patch.

"Maybe she changed her mind," Katy thought. She looked over and watched the other girls leave. They were all talking and laughing and holding up their patches to admire them. "I did try my hardest," Katy said to herself. "I can't help it if I'm not as good as the other girls. I did try. Really, I did." Miss Jenna came back outside. Katy could tell she was holding something.

"Here, Katy," Miss Jenna said, as she handed Katy a

lollipop. "Maybe you can get a patch next time, okay?" Katy nodded, turned, and began to walk away.

"Bye, Katy!" Miss Jenna called after her. Katy turned toward her teacher and waved. She would have said goodbye, but she knew that if she opened her mouth she would start crying. She just walked on, staring at her lollipop.

"A lollipop?" she mumbled. "Lollipops are for babies. I wanted a patch. I don't want a patch *next* time. I want a patch *this* time. All that time I spent at the lessons was for nothing. I really did try as hard as I could." Katy rinsed off in the shower room and put a T-shirt on over her swimming suit. She hung her head and walked to the main lobby of the building.

As Katy entered the lobby, she expected to see her mom, but didn't. Usually, when Katy came to the lobby, Mom was waiting in the brown minivan just outside the door, or sitting in the lobby reading a book. Her parents usually didn't leave Katy anywhere in public alone, but since they knew the owners of the pool and several of the teachers, Mom often ran errands while Katy had her lesson.

Katy looked outside, but she didn't see her mom

anywhere. She stood right up against the big windows with her swim bag in her hand and watched every car that drove by or pulled into the parking lot. Her other hand still clutched the lollipop. She looked down at it and two tears rolled slowly down her cheeks, followed by two more. She wiped the tears away and hoped that everyone would just think her face was wet from the pool.

Katy watched people coming in and leaving, but she saw no trace of her mom. The mailman came to put the day's mail in the large mailbox just outside the door. He looked straight at Katy and smiled, but Katy looked down so that he wouldn't see her crying. The tears were getting harder to hide.

Katy wondered if something had happened to her mom or if she had forgotten about picking her up. Just when Katy was about to go to the front desk and ask for permission to call her dad at work, she spotted the brown minivan and watched it pull up at the front of the building. Katy rushed outside. She opened the door of the van and jumped in.

"I didn't forget you, Katy," Mom began to explain immediately. "I was at the grocery store and when I realized it was almost time to leave and come pick you up, I hurried to the checkout. There was only one register open and several people were already in line ahead of me, so it took a long time. I'm so sorry."

"It's okay," Katy said. "It's not just because you're late that I'm upset. This has been one of the worst days of my whole life." Katy opened her hand and held out the lollipop for her mom to see.

"What's wrong with the lollipop?" Mom asked. "Don't you like strawberry?"

"I don't care what flavor it is," said Katy. "It's not that. Miss Jenna gave everybody else a patch with a red seahorse on it, but all she gave me was this lollipop." Katy proceeded to tell her mom all the details of the lesson, including slipping through Miss Jenna's arms in the deep end. "I really did try my hardest, Mom," Katy concluded.

"I know you did, Sweetie," Mom said, as she laid a hand on Katy's knee, "and I'm sure you did a good job. I'm sorry you didn't get the patch. I know you've been looking forward to it for weeks."

When the two of them reached home, Katy hurried through the kitchen, down the hall, and into her bedroom. She was glad that Anna was somewhere else. Katy closed the door. She dropped her swim bag, picked up Sugar Plum, and threw herself down on the bottom bunk. She let out all the tears she had been trying to hold back since the moment Miss Jenna handed the girl beside her the last patch with the red seahorse on it. Katy looked over at the wall above the fish tank and thought how empty it looked.

Before too long, Anna came in. Katy turned her face toward the wall. Anna walked over to Katy's bed and knelt down beside her little sister.

"I'm sorry you didn't get the patch," Anna said. There was a long pause when neither of them knew what to say. Anna began to gently scratch Katy's back. "Do you want to go up in the playhouse?" Anna asked. Katy shrugged, then nodded. She got up slowly and laid Sugar Plum beside her wet pillow, but then picked the doll up again and took her up into the closet playhouse with her. Katy made Sugar Plum sit beside her, leaning against the wall. Anna and Katy pulled out the paper and markers and began to draw.

"Just don't stand up," Anna said, looking at Katy with a grin. "There's a light bulb above your head!"

Katy looked up at the light bulb and couldn't help but smile. Anna drew another picture of the dog she dreamed of owning. Katy picked up the red marker and drew a seahorse.

17

Decision

For as long as Katy could remember, Thursday night was Family Night. A movie, a game, a special supper—whatever they did, the Porters were together, and that was the most important thing.

Katy remembered a few years ago when they all wrote down on little slips of paper things they would like to do on Family Night. They put them in a jar and pulled them out one by one. Katy was only about four years old and one of her suggestions was to play house, which they all did together one Thursday night.

On one of Seth's slips of paper, he wrote down "Monolopy." Dad thought that Seth had misspelled Monopoly, but when Seth's slip of paper was drawn, he explained. Monolopy was a new game he had invented.

You used the Monopoly board and cards, but there was a whole new set of rules. First of all, instead of going the usual way around the board, you went backwards, starting with Boardwalk and going around the other way. When you drew a card, it applied to yourself, the person to your right, and the person sitting next to the person on your left. When you rolled the dice, the bank paid you the amount of money equal to the dots on the dice. Double sixes was the best roll since it meant you received twelve dollars.

Seth had other complicated rules, and everyone else was constantly asking him what they had to do or what a certain roll meant. A roll of a five on one die and a two on the other always took you straight to the Electric Company. When you landed on St. Charles Place, everyone paid you five dollars. The game lasted for three and a half hours; and despite Seth's hard work making up the rules, they never played it again.

One of Anna's suggestions was to reminisce about embarrassing moments of the past. They laughed until they cried that night, remembering stories they had told before, and telling of new embarrassing moments.

It was Thursday night again. All of the Porters were

sitting in the den downstairs. Dad and Mom were beside each other on the couch. Anna was leaning her head on Mom's shoulder. Seth was sitting on the floor and Katy was in the big arm chair. The delicious smell of Mom's homemade pizza they had eaten for supper still lingered in the air.

"It's time to make a decision about school," Dad said. "Your mother and I will make the final decision, but we would like to know what each of you think. Seth, why don't you go first?"

Seth thought for a moment about what to say. "It's an interesting proposition," he said finally. "I'd like to give it a try."

"Is that all you want to say?" Mom asked.

"Yes," Seth replied, "at least for now."

"How about you, Anna?" said Dad.

"I think I'll miss school," Anna began, "but I think being homeschooled sounds neat. Earlier this summer I really didn't want to, but I've been praying about it, and I think it's the right thing for us to do. It might be hard at first, but I guess we'll get used to it. Would we do special projects and things?"

Mom nodded. "I've been thinking about lots of fun

projects we can do," she said. "We'll probably turn this room into the school room and do most of our work in here. Of course, there will be math and spelling and history and the other usual subjects; but with it being just us, we should be able to have plenty of time to go on field trips, go with Dad when he has a business trip, take time for craft projects, and lots of things like that."

"It sounds good to me," Anna finished. Everyone looked at Katy.

"I think it would be cool," she said. "Besides, lots of kids homeschool now. The public schools are in a pretty sorry state these days and homeschooling protects them from the evil influences of the world. Public schools are turning out too many children who are rebellious, disrespectful, and disobedient." They all laughed, and this time Katy didn't mind.

"It sounds like we're all together on this, and I am thankful for that," said Dad. "Mom and I have been praying that God would make us all want to do the same thing, whatever that might be. It sounds like He has answered that prayer and made us all want to homeschool. I thought your mom was a little crazy when she first suggested the idea of homeschooling you guys, but now I see that I'm the one who was crazy. I think it's a great idea and I think it's going to work out fine. Let's pray." The Porters bowed their heads and Dad asked God to bless the school year ahead.

Katy lay in bed that night, trying to imagine how homeschooling would really be. She thought it would be strange having her mom as her teacher, until she thought about how her mom already was her teacher. She had taught Katy about sewing and cooking, the Bible, and many other things. Katy wondered how it would be to spend her days with Anna and Seth instead of other kids her own age. Then she thought about how much fun she and Seth had playing marbles and how much she and Anna liked to play dress-up together. She decided that spending more time with them would be nice. She thought it sounded fun for them to work on math and spelling and history all in the same room and then have more time to play when the school work was finished.

Katy thought about her class last year. She thought about her friend Ruth, and missed her. She had enjoyed playing with Ruth at recess and taking care of a rolly-polly together. There had been good things last year in school that Katy would miss, but she knew there would be good things at home, too. She thought about the school building. It was big and old and not very pretty. Then she thought about home, and knew it was the place she wanted to be.

18

Blessed

Two weeks later, Katy was outside, swinging as hard as she could in the swing that hung from the crabapple tree in the front yard. Katy was happy and content as she pumped her legs back and forth.

"Thanks, God," she prayed, "for this tree and this swing and the world and Jesus. Thanks for Dad and Mom and Seth and Anna. I'm glad we get to start homeschooling next week. I think it will be fun. Thank You for loving me, Father." Katy pumped her legs harder and went as high as she could. She counted to ten and jumped out of the swing, landed on her feet, but then fell to her knees. She sprang back up onto her feet and picked up Sugar Plum, who had been lying on the ground nearby. Katy walked to the maple tree.

The step-ladder was nearby because it was Saturday and Dad had been working on the siding around the kitchen window. He was finished with the ladder now, so Katy brought it over to the tree. She climbed up the two steps and pulled herself up onto the lowest branch. She left Sugar Plum on the step-ladder. Katy climbed higher until she could see over their roof and across their back yard. She saw Mr. Robb, who lived in the house behind them, working in his garden. She saw Chinway playing tag with James in their yard.

"Hi, Chinway!" Katy called out.

"Time out, James," Katy heard Chinway say. "Where are you Katy?"

"I'm up here!" Katy called back. Chinway looked up and spotted Katy. She came over to the Porter's yard and stood under the maple tree. Katy climbed down to the lowest branch.

"Guess what, Chinway!" Katy said. "My mom and dad decided to homeschool after all. We're supposed to start next week."

"Really? You're lucky. I wish my mom would do that. I don't like school. Well, I can't stay because James is waiting for me on base. I'll see you later, Katy." Chinway ran back to her yard and resumed her game of tag with her little brother.

Katy watched Chinway and James play together. She rested her head on a branch and thought about what Chinway had said. Katy realized how blessed she was to have a mom and dad who were willing to homeschool her. She knew that her mom and dad loved her and wanted what was best for her. Chinway had said Katy was lucky, but Katy didn't believe in luck. She wasn't lucky; she was blessed. Katy knew that Chinway was blessed, too. Some of Chinway's blessings were the same as Katy's, and some were different. Chinway was loved by her parents, just like Katy was loved by hers. Being homeschooled wouldn't make Katy better than Chinway, and going to public school wouldn't make Chinway better than Katy. They were different, but Katy knew that being different was okay.

Katy heard a door open and close, and a moment later she heard Anna calling her name.

"I'm up here!" Katy called back. Anna came around to the front of the house and looked up into the tree.

"Would you like to go the Acorn Lady's?" Anna asked. "It's okay with Mom."

Katy beamed. "I'll be right down!" she called. Katy scrambled down the tree, quickly but carefully. Anna and Katy went into the garage to get their bikes. Katy's bike was blue with clouds on the seat. It had a white plastic basket strapped to the front of it. The two sisters rode down the sidewalk, Katy in front. The Acorn Lady lived at the far end of their street. The ground in front of her house was covered with acorns. Anna and Katy began gathering the acorns and dropping them into the basket on Katy's bike.

"Thanks, Anna," Katy said, "for coming with me."

Anna smiled. "Sure," she said, "it's fun." When the basket was full, the girls rode back to their house. They went the long route, though, all the way around the block, enjoying the glorious afternoon. Katy waved at Chinway and James as she rode past their house. She was proud of the fact that she could ride her bike with just one hand, so she waved for a long time.

When they reached their house, Anna and Katy scattered some of the acorns across the driveway and rode their bikes over them, smashing them for the squirrels. Seth came outside and started shooting hoops. They all three laughed when a plastic ball came soaring over the house from the back yard. It was the ball Seth had hit onto the roof the night they were locked out of the house. Dad had finally gotten around to retrieving it from the gutter.

Sugar Plum still sat on the step-ladder under the maple tree that shaded Seth, Anna, and Katy as they played. Sugar Plum stared at them with big blue eyes and a smile that would never go away. Right at that moment, Katy felt that her own smile would never go away, either.

Author's Note

The story of Katy is based on memories of my own childhood. Urbana, Illinois, was my home, as it is Katy's. A swing hung from the crabapple tree in our front yard and the Acorn Lady lived down the street. My sister and I played for countless hours with our dress-up box in the basement, drew pictures in our little attic closet, and played in the playhouse in the back yard; and I collected baseball cards because my brother did. My dad and I used to play basketball on the driveway and I still have the owl my mom and I made with the felt beak and button eyes. Irene had us over to play croquet many times and there really was a mouse in the church oven. My parents never actually locked us out, but some friends of ours accidentally did that when I was a little older and babysitting their kids!

It was fun to remember all these things and so much more as I wrote Katy's story. I was blessed to grow up with parents who love God, love each other, and love their children. I am very thankful that they made the decision to homeschool my siblings and me. My brother and sister and I shared many happy times together and became great friends as we grew up. I have had many wonderful friends through the years, some of whom are portrayed as characters in Katy's story. Like Katy, I know that I am blessed.

Mary Evelyn

Also available from
Notgrass History:

Katy's Box

It's time for a new adventure! Katy Porter is nervous and excited about beginning her first year of homeschooling. The day before school starts, Katy asks her dad if she can keep the empty box he is about to throw away. Katy puts keepsakes from her past inside the box, such as an old necklace and a rock she brought back from the ocean. Katy tucks the box safely under her bed, but the box is not full.

Will the coming year bring good times with her family and fun new treasures to add to her box? Or will homeschooling be just a big stack of boring hard work?

Katy's Box is a story of learning and of learning what matters.